Kitty felt dizzy and weak and leaned against the side of the cabin for support. The boards creaked only slightly, but Montfort leaped to his feet, quickly grabbing up a short-bladed knife that lay beside him. Kitty cringed against the side of the painted boards, trying to make herself invisible.

Slowly, carefully, Montfort brought the knife down. "I'm sorry, Miss Walsingham," he said. He came closer and took her hand. She looked up at him and started to say something, but the words never came. He came closer and closer, almost, but not quite touching her, a strange look in his amber eyes. From a distance, Kitty heard the sound of the knife hitting the deck. Then, slowly, almost cautiously, he touched the side of her face with his fingertips. Before she knew what was happening, he had drawn her close to him, and his mouth was on hers . . .

WIVES, LIES AND DOUBLE LIVES

MISTRESSES ($4.50, 17-109)
By Trevor Meldal-Johnsen
Kept women. Pampered females who have everything: designer clothes, jewels, furs, lavish homes. They are the beautiful mistresses of powerful, wealthy men. A mistress is a man's escape from the real world, always at his beck and call. There is only one cardinal rule: *do not fall in love*. Meet three mistresses who live in the fast lane of passion and money, and who know that one wrong move can cost them everything.

ROYAL POINCIANA ($4.50, 17-179)
By Thea Coy Douglass
By day she was Mrs. Madeline Memory, head housekeeper at the fabulous Royal Poinciana. Dressed in black, she was a respectable widow and the picture of virtue. By night she the French speaking "Madame Memphis", dressed in silks and sipping champagne with con man Harrison St. John Loring. She never intended the game to turn into true love . . .

WIVES AND MISTRESSES ($4.95, 17-120)
By Suzanne Morris
Four extraordinary women are locked within the bitterness of a century old rivalry between two prominent Texas families. These heroines struggle against lies and deceptions to unlock the mysteries of the past and free themselves from the dark secrets that threaten to destroy both families.

Available wherever paperbacks are sold, or order direct from the Publisher. Send cover price plus 50¢ per copy for mailing and handling to Pinnacle Books, Dept. 17-415, 475 Park Avenue South, New York, N.Y. 10016. Residents of New York, New Jersey and Pennsylvania must include sales tax. DO NOT SEND CASH.

Sweet Deceit

DAWN ALDRIDGE POORE

PINNACLE BOOKS
WINDSOR PUBLISHING CORP.

PINNACLE BOOKS

are published by

Windsor Publishing Corp.
475 Park Avenue South
New York, NY 10016

Copyright © 1990 Dawn Aldridge Poore

All rights reserved. No part of this book may be reproduced in any form or by any means without the prior written consent of the Publisher, excepting brief quotes used in reviews.

First printing: October, 1990

Printed in the United States of America

Chapter One

"Good God, Kitty! Wherever are you going? Here I find you sneaking out the door in the middle of the night." Thomas stopped and looked at her in amazement. "And you ain't even wearing your bonnet!"

Miss Kitty Walsingham stopped in the act of softly closing the big front door behind her and looked up in horror at her brother. "Ssshh, Thomas," she said, looking quickly around. "You'll wake everyone."

"Really?" He lifted an elegant eyebrow and gently pushed her back into the house. "I think you'd better go inside. You'll catch your death of cold out here."

"Don't be silly," she snapped. "By the way, what are *you* doing out so late? It must be after midnight."

"Actually, it's around one," Thomas said lazily. "And you should know better than to ask a gentleman where he's been."

"I do know better, but I don't see any gentlemen around."

Thomas laughed. "Touché. Now, dear Kit, tell me, where were you going?" he asked, lighting a branch of candles from the sconce in the hall.

"Ssshh." Kitty looked around the cavernous front hall to see if anyone had heard. "Let's go in the library and I'll tell you," she whispered, moving down the hall. "Just be quiet."

To her surprise, Thomas followed without a word,

closing the library door behind him. He set the branch of candles down on the heavy desk and looked at her. "Not eloping, are you, Kitty? That's not at all the thing, you know. Who is he, by the way?"

"Eloping? Thomas, don't be such a blathering goose," Kitty said. "Now for heaven's sake will you hush and put out that branch of candles? Do you want them to see you?" She dashed over to the window and peered out, hiding behind the heavy drapes.

"Them who?" Thomas asked in a voice loud enough to wake the dead. "Ssshh," Kitty hissed, but Thomas, as usual, appeared not to notice her. "Them?" he said again. "Kitty, you ain't running away with more than one, are you?" he asked, aghast. "My God, Kit!"

Kitty snatched the branch of candles from his fingers and blew out the flames, leaving them only the moonlight to see by. "Thomas," she said, trying in vain to keep the irritation from her voice. "I'm not running away with anyone. As I told you quite plainly in London, I plan to marry Richard." She paused guiltily as her brother stared at her. "Even though he doesn't know it yet, I'm sure he'll be as delighted as I am."

Thomas gave her a lazy smile. "I just want to be notified when you tell him. Better yet, I'd like to know what his father's going to say."

"Thomas, that doesn't signify right now." She gave her brother a withering look. "Sometimes I can understand perfectly well why Cambridge gave up on your education."

He was visibly annoyed. "Dash it, Kitty, I wish you'd quit casting aspersions on my intelligence."

"I would never do that, Thomas," she answered sweetly. "I merely cast aspersions on your *lack* of intelligence."

"You're just jealous," Thomas said.

"I've never been jealous in my life."

Thomas chuckled. "No? Who used to scream and fight whenever needlework or tatting was mentioned? Who used to rag at Papa for hours because she couldn't go to the university?"

Kitty grimaced before she could stop herself. "Quit acting superior, Thomas. It doesn't become you."

"You never give up, do you, Kit?" He was laughing again.

"Never." She peered out the window as she spoke. Suddenly she stiffened. "Look, Thomas! There they are again. There!"

His gaze followed the direction of her pointed finger. "Don't see a thing, Kitty." He squinted and got close to the glass, his breath clouding the panes completely.

Biting back a comment, she rubbed the pane with her fingers to clear it. "There! That light. Did you see it?" She pointed to the spot where there had been a quick flash of light, much like that from a quickly shuttered lantern.

"Probably somebody out walking late or maybe smugglers," Thomas said with a shrug. "After all, Kit, when you live on the coast like we do, and with things the way they are with all these rumours floating around about Boney, what else can you expect?" A flash of knowledge hit him and he stared at her. "Good God, Kitty! You weren't going out there to . . . to . . . to *investigate?*"

"I most certainly was, Thomas. And what's more, I'm still going to do it." She stared defiantly at him.

"Kitty." It was a strangled sound. "It just ain't *done!*"

"No one's going to know, Thomas, and if you're so worried, you can come with me. I'll make sure no smugglers get you."

Thomas sat heavily in a red damask chair and regarded his sister, then took flint and lit two of the can-

7

dles. "You can't do it," he said heavily. "I'll go tell Papa if you try."

"You wouldn't!"

"Try me."

Kitty stared at him and then sat down in the opposite chair with a petulant frown. "Where's your sense of adventure, Thomas? I would have thought Cambridge and your trek through the Levant would have given you a feel for such things. Surely, the past season in London can't have turned you into a dandy and a fop."

"Certainly not!" Thomas was indignant. "I just happen to know better than to rush off at all hours of the night after a smuggler or whatever. It just ain't done, Kitty. If you know something for sure, call the constable."

"Thomas." Kitty paused to marshal her reasons and to give her voice a calm tone. "How can I call for the constable when I have no evidence? I must go see what's going on. *Then* I can call for the constable."

Thomas shook his head. "Can't do it, Kit."

Kitty snorted. "Well, I see your time in London *has* made you think you're one of the dandified *ton*."

"A man can acquire a bit of polish in a short time, Kit."

Kitty snorted. "Feathers! I've just been in France for two months, and I know you're still the same dunderhead you were when I left. Are you going with me or not?"

"Not." Thomas got what Kitty had always termed his "bulldog" look. She knew it was useless to talk to him. "All right, Thomas, if it will soothe your newfound sense of propriety, I'll go on to bed like a child."

"Fine, but I'm going to lock you in." He smiled sweetly at her.

"You wouldn't *dare!*" This was doing it up too

brown, even for a bothersome brother like Thomas.

He gave her his lazy smile again. "I know you too well, Kitty. You never give up that easily. I'd wager the minute I turned my back, you'd be off and running down to the shingle. Except this time you'd probably break your neck trying to dangle from your bedchamber window on a bedsheet." He leaned back in his chair and folded his arms. "Ain't I right, now?"

Kitty glared at him and refused to answer.

"I knew it!" he said triumphantly. "I can read you like a book, sister mine." He glanced out the window again. "There's nothing out there anyway, and even if there is, it's probably Montfort."

"Montfort?" Kitty was blank.

"Forgot you didn't know. A good many things happened while you were visiting Grand-mère." Thomas stretched his legs out in front of him and smiled, savoring his superior knowledge. It wasn't often he got to tell his sister something. "Captain Montfort, you know."

"No, I don't know," Kitty said waspishly, "and I wish you'd quit dawdling and tell me. You know you're dying to."

She was quite right about Thomas, as usual. He gave up all pretense of ennui. "James Montfort, the second son of the earl of Sobey. He's a real war hero and, let me tell you, Kit, he's all the crack in London. He belongs to all the clubs, and has the sweetest pair of goers you've ever seen. A pair of matched ebonies, not a white hair on 'em. And silver trimmed harness." Thomas stretched again and smiled as if he had related everything one needed to know.

"And . . . ," Kitty prompted.

Thomas came out of his reverie, his mind still on Montfort's skill with the ribbons. "You should just see him, Kitty. I once saw him race down the Bristol road with Francis Brentwood. You never saw anything like it. He took a corner right in front of me like it had a feathered edge. It was something to see."

Kitty ground her teeth in exasperation and tried to remain calm. "Just what is Montfort doing here, Thomas? Surely he hasn't come down to race by the sea."

"Oh no, Kit, nothing like that. He's bought the Tillbury's place next door."

"He *what?*" Kitty's voice was almost a screech. She caught herself and looked around to make sure no one had heard her.

"He's bought out Tillbury's estate. The whole five hundred acres, manor house and all. Lock, stock, and barrel. I think he's even going to rename it."

"I can't believe it. I've been home for three days and no one told me that Sherbourne's been sold. And to some high-in-the-instep dandy from London!" Kitty pondered this information. "I imagine that he won't even want us riding through there."

Thomas shrugged. "Oh, I don't think he'll mind. He came over here the other day and asked if we would mind him riding along the beach and maybe mooring a boat there until he can get a proper dock built over at Sherbourne. He won't mind us over there. Tit for tat, you know. He seemed like a right sort."

Kitty sniffed at the expression on Thomas's face. He obviously had a bad case of misplaced hero worship. "Why do you think Montfort might be on the beach at this time of night, Thomas?" she asked, getting back to the reason Thomas had discovered her getting ready to slip out the front door after midnight.

"I don't know, but if he's down there, I'm sure he has a good reason." Thomas looked at her, then smiled. "How was your trip?"

"Are you deliberately changing the subject, Thomas?"

Thomas smiled his lazy smile at her. It was his most charming feature, and he knew the effect it had on the various women in his life. It worked nicely with ladies of dubious reputation, it accomplished wonders with Maman, but had little effect on Kitty. "Not at all, Kit. We just haven't had a chance to talk since you came home, and I was wondering just how you got on. How was Grandmère?"

"Fine. Tell me about Montfort."

"Dash it all, Kit, there's nothing to tell. He's just decided to settle down and came down here to remodel Tillbury's estate. I don't know anything else about him except what I just told you." He paused. "Except I heard it from Basset at the club that Harriette Marlowe has been on the dangle for him, and it's just a matter of time until there's an announcement in the *Courier*." He glared at her. "Most men do want to settle down, you know."

"Harriette Marlowe." Kitty said the words through thinned lips. "I would prefer that you not mention that name in my presence, Thomas."

To her chagrin, Thomas laughed aloud. "She did do you up one with that boy of Humber's. Snatched him right out from under your nose, didn't she?"

Kitty rose regally. "I don't recall that she *snatched* Alfred. I had already decided to give him his congé." She glared down at Thomas, daring him to say anything else. Thomas paid her no attention.

"No, Kit, *snatched* is the word. But, my girl, you're better off. Take it from a big brother, that milksop wasn't for you."

"He evidently wasn't for Harriette Marlowe either, if she's about to catch a diamond like Montfort." She paused. "Besides, you know Richard and I have an

11

understanding."

Thomas had the poor grace to guffaw loudly, while Kitty cringed, knowing the whole household would awaken. She bit back a retort as he stood and escorted her to the door. "Some understanding. Poor Richard don't even know about it. Besides, you only remembered it when Alfred left you standing. Very convenient. But then, Richard always did come in handy."

"Do you know you're a boor and a peasant?"

"You've told me more than once." He paused and looked at his sister. "Go to bed. If you try to get out of the house, I swear I'll wake Papa and come after you with the whole house in tow. I mean it. If you *must* satisfy your curiosity, tomorrow we'll walk down to the beach and look around. I'm sure you won't see anything."

"By tomorrow, I'm very sure I won't see anything," she answered acidly. "Very well, Thomas. I'll go to bed." She pulled the door behind her. "This time," she added.

Thomas stared at the closed door for a moment and then poured himself a small glass of sherry. Damme, if his sister wasn't all grown up now. He had been surprised when he first saw her when she got back from France. She had just been gone two months or so, just since the peace with France, but it seemed that she had left a girl and returned a grown woman. But then, he thought to himself as he drank his sherry and poured another, Kit always was unpredictable.

And what about her taking off for the beach in the dead of the night? Every other girl would have fainted instead, but then, Kitty always was a headstrong little thing; Papa used to joke that Kitty should have been the son of the family. Thomas saw beyond the joke and realized it was true. Kitty had been the one to ride hard and rush her fences, always the one who went first while Thomas followed.

But times had changed, now. He was a man and Kitty was, well, she was a headstrong hoyden who needed a man to rein her in. Damme, he thought to himself, Kitty must be one and twenty. He would have to remind Papa to do something about her.

He sat up quickly as an idea hit him. Maybe he should go ahead and invite Richard down for a few weeks. That should do the trick. After all, as Kit had mentioned, there *had* been an understanding—Richard had offered for her when he was ten and as far as Thomas knew, he still might. Richard had always been partial to Kitty. What the man saw in a scatter-brained, headstrong girl like Kit was a mystery, but then Richard was different, not much concerned with appearances. Might even be good for Richard, Thomas mused. After all, he was all wrapped up in the new agriculture theories lately, trying to impress his father with his running of the estates. Might just do Richard good to get out a bit.

Thomas smiled broadly, sat down at the big walnut desk, and reached for quill and paper.

Chapter Two

Kitty got up at her usual early hour and waited impatiently for Thomas. Evidently he was still keeping London hours. By ten o'clock, she could stand no more. She decided to go on by herself. She was wearing her new sprigged muslin, but then remembering her errand, she decided it would be best to change into something plainer. She settled on an old, frayed, and too tight round gown and her pattens. One glance in her mirror told her Grandmère would be scandalized, but this errand was no place for frivolity. Snatching up an old shawl that needed mending, she set off for the beach.

It was one of her favorite walks. For her there was no place in the world quite like Bellevoir. She enjoyed traveling to London for a while during the season, seeing her friends in the *ton*, and going to parties, but when she was there, she often found herself longing to return to the sight and sounds of the sea. The moods of the water, the clouds, and the winds always seemed to draw her back to Bellevoir.

She paused and took a deep breath of the salt-tinged air. It was wonderful to be back home. She had been gone since the peace had been signed, accompanying her grandmother back to France. Grandmère had gone back home as soon as possible after Napoleon had been exiled, and Kitty had gone along to help her settle in. Perhaps I should have stayed a little longer, Kitty thought with guilt, but I missed England. Besides, Grandmère no longer needed her company now that she was settled in her chateau and had rejoined her old friends in Brittany. Grandmère had stayed at Bellevoir with them during the war, but she never cared for the English coast. Often Kitty had seen her gazing longingly in the direction of France. "It will be over before long, Grandmère," she would tell the old lady, not really believing it herself as the war dragged on. Now to almost everyone's surprise, it was over. Napoleon, the invincible, the man who could not be defeated, had been and now had been exiled.

But still, there were already rumors that he was planning to return. Kitty had heard them both in France and here in the village. Surely not, Kitty thought. With Napoleon, there were always rumors. It had been that way as long as she could remember.

She shrugged off the thoughts of Napoleon and politics to concentrate on the shingled beach. Walking slowly, concentrating on the edge of the shingle, she found the imprints of hooves. Someone had been riding this way, probably early this morning. Picking up something from the smugglers, most likely, she thought. If only Thomas hadn't happened upon her right at that moment, she might have found out something exciting. She had heard tales of smugglers all her life, and it was a known fact that there were dozens of them operating between here and France, although she had never seen one. Kitty had no thought what she would do if she found a smuggler; she certainly had no intention of turning one over to a magistrate. If anything, the smuggler was probably a close neighbor.

She was absently following the tracks of the horse

when they suddenly disappeared in a wash. She stopped and looked around, but could see nothing. No tracks on the other side, no tracks returning. There had to be something. She went up one side of the wash, crossing at low water.

After much examination, she found nothing at all. Now here was a *real* mystery. Wait until she told Thomas. He'd be sorry he hadn't come down last night. She started to recross the wash, but the water had begun to come up, and it was much deeper. There was only one thing left to do — she took a deep breath and leaped. After all, she'd jumped this same wash a thousand times over the years. This time, however, her patten slipped and she landed on the side of her foot. For a moment, it was touch and go, but then she fell straight backwards into the water with a splash, filling her face and mouth with sandy salt water. It was so cold she caught her breath and began using some words she had heard the stableboys say, words that no proper young lady should ever use.

She shook her head angrily as she righted herself and wiped the muddy water and sand from her face. "Damme," she muttered.

"My sentiments, exactly." The voice was a low drawl.

Kitty shoved her muddy hair from her eyes and squinted upwards at the stranger on the large black horse. He and the horse belonged together, she thought. He was dark, not handsome in the conventional sense, his face was too dark for that, but his cheekbones were high, and his lips were thin and had an arrogant smile on them. His hair was a dark chestnut that glinted with gold highlights in the sun.

"Who are you?" Kitty asked rudely. She dragged her sodden skirts from the mud and stood before him, dripping.

He got down easily from the horse. "I might ask the same of you. Has your mistress sent you on some errand and you've lost your way?"

"My mistress?" It took Kitty a moment to realize that he had mistaken her for a serving girl. She haughtily drew herself up to her full height, which, to her chagrin, was about even with his shoulders. She still had to look up at him. "Sir, you mistake yourself. I happen to live here at Bellevoir. Now if you will be so good as to explain exactly what you are doing riding on *our* beach . . ." She let her words trail off as his dark amber eyes examined her, taking in every detail from her muddy, wet hair, down to the sodden hem of her gown still swirling in the water of the wash.

"Ah, I see. My apologies. If you live at Bellevoir, then you must be the delectable Miss Walsingham," he said with an elaborate bow and more than a touch of sarcasm in his voice.

"Exactly," she snapped, as realization hit her. "And you must be the insufferable Captain Montfort." She could have bitten her tongue as soon as the words were out.

He merely smiled at her. "Exactly," he said.

Kitty, for the first time in her life, was at a complete loss for words. She wanted to turn and flee, but no Walsingham had ever run, unless one counted a black sheep back in the fourteenth century, and everyone carefully refrained from mentioning him. There was little she could do except the pretty. She gritted her teeth and spoke. "I'm pleased to make your acquaintance, Captain Montfort," she said stiffly, extending a very muddy hand and stepping as regally as possible out of the water.

"As am I, Miss Walsingham," he said, again giving her a bow. He took her hand and stared at it as mud fell off in his palm. "I have heard of your loveliness from your brother, but, upon closer inspection, I do not believe he has done you justice." The corner of his mouth trembled as he tried to suppress a laugh.

Kitty longed to throw sand on him. However, years of Grand-mère's training came to her rescue. "Thank you, Captain Montfort," she said haughtily, speaking through the sand on her lips. "I'm sure Thomas and my parents are looking forward to having you visit. Now," she withdrew her hand, leaving, she noted with great satisfaction, sea water and sand dripping from his fingers, "I really must get home. It's been a pleasure to meet you."

"Thank you for your invitation, Miss Walsingham." Kitty looked up with a snap of her head. She didn't recall issuing any invitation, but Montfort continued smoothly, "I can only hope your appearance at my visit lives up to this introduction." He looked at her with amusement as he shook mud from his hand.

Kitty glared at him, wished she could use a word to describe him that the stableboy had used to describe a recalcitrant horse, then thought the better of it. Without a word, she turned and, dragging her muddy skirts behind her, sloshed up the shingle.

To her total chagrin, she heard him laughing heartily behind her as he mounted his horse.

"A truly terrible man," she fumed a short while later to Thomas. He had been eating when she came in, and she had dared him to speak to her until she had bathed and changed. He was lying in wait for her in the library when she came down, and, although she tried to hedge, she had been forced to relate the whole sordid story. To her great annoyance, Thomas enjoyed it thoroughly.

"I can't imagine what you find remarkable in Montfort, Thomas," she said primly, trying to salvage her dignity. "Harriette Marlowe is certainly welcome to him, although what she would ever want with him is beyond me. The man has no conduct at all."

Thomas laughed at her. "No conduct. That word from you about a paragon of the *ton*." He stopped and mopped ineffectually at his eyes. "Oh, my Lord, it was worth my quarter's allowance to see you coming in the door. What a bedraggled looking specimen! That seaweed in your hair was just the right touch." He went off again into gales of laughter.

"Trust you to join forces with that odious creature," she snapped as she went out the door. Thomas was still laughing.

Kitty ate heartily, then spent the remainder of the day fuming, thinking of witty things she wished she had said to Montfort. Her father, sensing her downcast mood, suggested a ride in the late afternoon. "I need to get out, Kitty, and you haven't ridden Beau since you got back from France. I know the grooms have been exercising him, but it isn't the same."

"You're right, Papa. I went down to see him and took him an apple. He needs a ride as much as I."

There was even a new habit to wear. Grand-mère had insisted that she get one, a gray trimmed with black braid in the new Cossack manner. Kitty had thought the material would not become her, but as usual, Grand-mère had been right. When Kitty put it on, the severe cut of the gray emphasized her trim figure, making a straight fall from the jacket trimmed with braid and frogs. There was a spill of dove-colored lace at the neck and sleeves. Grand-mère had even insisted on a hat of gray with a black feather. Kitty didn't stop to ask herself why she was dressing so for a romp in the country.

"We should be parading in Hyde Park, instead of riding by the cottages of the village," her papa said when he saw her. "You look lovely, my dear."

Kitty kissed him quickly. "Thank you, Papa. So do you."

The ride was just what she had needed, Kitty thought, as she reined in Beau and looked out over the Channel. "I know now how Grandmère felt," she said to her father as he paused beside her on his big gray. "While I was in France, all I could think of was getting back home. I wonder if Maman is ever homesick that way."

"She was at first, but she and Grandmère were so relieved to have escaped the Terror that she settled in. Besides, this part of the country strongly resembles Quimper. You know your mother has always preferred the country." Kitty noticed a small smile on her father's face. In truth, it had been such a love match between her father and mother that either of them was happy anywhere the other was. Kitty had loved to hear the story of how they had met during the French Revolution and how brave her father had been in rescuing the Brissac family and bringing them to England.

Maman had been perfectly happy, but Grandmère had been homesick for Brittany. Kitty could understand this now since, while she had been with Grandmère, beautiful as Quimper had been, she had longed to return to Bellevoir. "Ah, my child," Grandmère had complained, "I fear you have become all English." Kitty had laughed, but she had known that Grandmère, as usual, was right.

"Papa," she asked, a frown on her face as she looked toward France, "do you think it's really over? Is Napoleon really finished?"

Jerome Walsingham shook his head. "I hope so,

Kitty. The peace has been signed and Louis returned to France, but there are already rumors that Napoleon is planning an escape from exile."

"I know, I heard them in France." She paused. "I even heard them in the village yesterday when I went down. Mr. Braithwaite was talking to someone and saying that it would be good if Napoleon were emperor again."

"Braithwaite!" her father said with a touch of disgust. "Of course he would think so. The man has made money supplying troops with arms. He'd like to see men slaughtered forever."

Kitty's eyes widened. "I didn't know that, Papa. How terrible for Barbara." Kitty thought about Braithwaite's daughter, a shy, homely girl who seldom had anything to say, but spent every minute she had been at Bellevoir staring worshipfully at Thomas.

"She isn't responsible for her father," Papa answered. "Still, men like Braithwaite will always exist, and always want a war to go on."

"Do you think it's over?"

He looked at her. "I hope so. We all need some breathing space. Still, I won't lie to you, Catherine, I do worry about Napoleon. I'm not sure that exile is the answer to his ambition."

"I hope he stays on Elba. I'm so tired of the war." Kitty looked wistfully at her father, and he felt a surge of guilt and remorse. Perhaps, he thought, now that Grandmère was back in France and the situation on the coast was quiet, there could be a real London season for her. A real come-out that would do justice to his beautiful daughter with the flyaway dark auburn hair and green eyes. He would arrange it as soon as possible. Rather than mention it to Kitty, he smiled to reassure her. "We're all tired of the war. No one was more glad to see Napoleon exiled than I." He patted her hand. "Shall we race along the beach?"

Before he could say more, Kitty was off on Beau, her sturdy little black that could run like the sea wind. Kitty loved rides along the edge of the sea, Beau's hooves splashing in the margin of the surf, the wind in her hair, and the taste of salt air on her tongue. Her hat fell back, held only by its ribbons, and tendrils of her hair began blowing in the wind as she rode. She finally pulled up near the wash below the house as her father caught up with her.

A smile lit his features. "At least I know one part of you is all English. You ride like all the Walsinghams."

Kitty laughed. "Someone has to make up for Thomas." It was a sore point with her father that Thomas had no seat at all. He was good enough with the ribbons, but the famed Walsingham ability to ride had somehow skipped him.

The sound of hooves coming along the beach stopped her father's reply, and they both turned to see the big black stallion of Montfort's pounding up the beach with his rider firmly guiding the large animal. He reined up beside them. His cool gaze on Kitty brought warmth to her cheeks.

"Ah, Montfort. It's good to see you today." Kitty glanced at her father, surprised by his warm greeting.

"Walsingham." His gaze flicked again to Kitty. "And is this your lovely daughter whom Thomas has been telling me about?"

Kitty was amazed. Surely her father wasn't on such good terms with this brazen high-in-the-instep fop. She took another look at him as her father made the introductions. Unfortunately, he didn't look at all like a fop, and he looked almost too much at home talking to her father. Kitty's jaw almost dropped as she heard her father extend an invitation for Montfort to join them for the evening. Even worse, Montfort accepted with alacrity.

"Until tonight, then," he said with a smile and a nod. Before he left them, Kitty blushed as he bid her adieu with a wicked, knowing grin as he glanced from her to the muddy wash. "Please be careful crossing the wash, Miss Walsingham. Ladies have been known to fall into the water."

Kitty bit back a retort as he rode away.

"I don't like that man," she said to her father.

He was surprised. "You've only just met him, Kitty. He seems a perfectly fine sort. Besides, I knew his father well, and I'm also acquainted with his older brother."

"Just who is he anyway? I don't recall a Montfort when I was in London."

Sir Jerome turned his horse's head and began a leisurely pace toward Bellevoir. "He's Sobey's second son. Perhaps you recall meeting his older brother. I believe I presented him to you at the Duchess of Sansbury's rout. Do you remember?"

Kitty wrinkled her brow in concentration. "Yes, I do recall. He succeeded to the title year before last, and married that Miss Langley from Winchester." She searched her memory for details. "He doesn't look at all like Montfort though. If I recall correctly, the earl is very blonde and slight."

"Looks like his mother, I've been told. Montfort favors the old earl." They rode on in companionable silence for a short time.

"Why wasn't Montfort in London as well?" Kitty finally asked, curiosity getting the better of her. Thomas had always said she was too curious for her own good, but then, what did Thomas know?

Her father glanced at her, surprised at her curiosity, but answered it without question. "I understand Montfort was army-mad when he was younger, and the earl bought him a commission—the Light Dragoons, I think. I've been told that he was an excellent soldier and commander, distinguished himself in the field if reports are to be believed."

Kitty smiled with satisfaction. "I knew he was a soldier, I just *knew* it. He's too arrogant to be anything else."

Her father looked at her in surprise before he started laughing. "It's true," Kitty said indignantly. "Anyone could see it."

"Perhaps," her father answered with a chuckle.

Kitty waited a few moments as they rode in silence. "Then what?" she prompted.

"What?" Sir Jerome looked at her. "Oh, what happened to Montfort then? He did well in the army, but then he was severely wounded and came home early this year to recover. Napoleon was exiled before he could return. Evidently, being wounded took most of the charm out of army life, so he sold out and decided to settle down."

"And just happened to pick out Sherbourne as the ideal place," Kitty said acidly.

"As a matter of fact, I'm responsible for that," Papa said.

Kitty couldn't believe her ears. "How?"

"I was in London and saw his brother at some function or other. He remarked that Montfort was looking for a quiet place on the coast and, since I knew Tillbury was looking for a buyer, I recommended Sherbourne. It's an ideal place to recuperate."

"He certainly seems to have recovered nicely," Kitty commented sarcastically as they approached the stables. "I think he's an odious man."

Her father stared at her and then chuckled, just like Thomas. Annoyed, Kitty went into the house without waiting for him.

Chapter Three

Kitty did not relish having Montfort over to dine, but she certainly could not fly in the face of her father's invitation, however unwarranted. She was still smouldering when she told Thomas about her second meeting with the captain.

"I'm convinced that there's something sinister about him," she said, as Thomas made a sound distinctly like a snort. Kitty glared at him and ignored the rudeness. "You can say what you wish, Thomas, and it won't signify, because I know you're overly impressed with him. But I'm telling you that there's something underhanded about that man. Why, just why, would he keep riding up and down our beach unless he were up to something?"

"Perhaps he needs to exercise his horse," Thomas suggested. "Or even perhaps he needs the fresh salt air. He *was* wounded, you know."

"Yes, yes, I heard." Kitty began pacing the small yellow parlor. "The camouflage of a wounded but loyal war hero would be the perfect disguise, you must admit." She paused in her pacing. "It would even be so perfect that a war wound could be feigned. He looks perfectly healthy to me."

"Dash it all, Kitty. Here you go off on one of your idiotic, harebrained tangents again." Thomas stood up. "I'm telling you that Montfort's a dashed good chap, and I'll listen to no more of this cockamamie drivel about him doing something underhanded and sinister. You've been reading one too many of those gothic novels."

"Nonsense," Kitty retorted at his retreating back. Still, she was stung. Gothic novels, indeed! Thomas should know her better than that. *He* was always the one going off chasing windmills. There was something about Montfort, she knew it. There was nothing concrete she could show Thomas—not yet, at least—but she had this feeling, and over the years, she had learned to trust her feelings. "Well," she muttered to herself, "if Thomas is too tame to help me, I'll just have to discover what I can by myself. Let Thomas be surprised then!" She squared her shoulders and went upstairs to prepare for the visitor. It didn't hurt to look as fashionable as possible when one was trying to extract information.

Kitty heard Duff, the butler, open the door and close it just as Bidwell was putting the finishing touches on her coiffure. She looked in the mirror and smiled in satisfaction. She wasn't one of those simpering blondes so currently in fashion, but as Grandmère had often told her, her face had character. Only in the last year had she realized how striking her coloring was, and she had bought all her new dresses to accent it. Now her green eyes glowed in the reflection of the emerald satin she wore, and the gold underslip complemented her skin. Bidwell had dressed her auburn curls around her face and had caught them up in the back with a riband and golden clip. Kitty was satisfied. She had never wished to be one of those milksop blondes, no matter how fashionable. They were always simpering around and acting stupid or else falling all over the floors with the vapors while every gentleman within distance hovered over them with burnt feathers or some such. Kitty loathed such histrionics, although she had to admit grudgingly that some used such ploys to great advantage. Harriette Marlowe, for one, came to mind.

She made a face in the mirror as she thought of the name, then forced the thought out of her mind and concentrated on her appearance. She adjusted the lace at the neckline of her gown and inspected herself one last time. "Very good, Bidwell," she told the dresser, and started down the stairs, trying to remember everything Grand-mère had told her about holding her head high and walking regally. Unfortunately, she tripped and almost fell at the bottom of the steps.

"Well, Kit, I have to say that you know how to make an entrance," Thomas said as she staggered into him. "Much more effective than merely saying 'How ye do?' Or have I been away from London too long and this is the latest thing?"

Kitty straightened up and stared at him. "Thomas, one of these days I'm going to land you a facer, I promise."

He laughed. "Now, Kit, you know ladies ought not say those things." He held his arm for her. "But then, I've never thought you fit the description of a lady anyway."

With a frown, Kitty took his arm and went down the hallway, thinking up a suitable rejoinder. Since she wasn't sure if she had been insulted or complimented by her brother, she came up with nothing before they reached the salon.

Montfort was already there, seated on the blue sofa next to Maman. He was again dressed in black and reminded Kitty of nothing so much as a large black crow ready to pounce. Kitty had to restrain herself from going over and sitting between him and her mother. Her mother seemed not to notice, and sat chattering away in her French-accented English that everyone found so charming.

"Ah, do come in, my dear," she said, motioning to Kitty. "Have you met my daughter?" she asked Montfort.

"I have already had the pleasure," he said with a smile at Kitty which she did not return.

At her mother's quizzing glance, Kitty explained. "I met Captain Montfort when I was riding with Papa."

"Ah, I see," Maman said with a smile. "Captain Montfort, you must come over often and go riding with Catherine now that she is back home. She is what you English call a 'bruising rider,' so no one here can keep up with her except her father, and he is often too busy to ride with her. I'm sure she would enjoy the company."

Kitty gritted her teeth as Captain Montfort smiled benignly at this invitation. "I'd be more than delighted. I enjoy a good ride every day, and I would consider it an honor to have such company." He looked at her with a wicked gleam in his eyes. "Tomorrow morning, Miss Walsingham?"

There was a moment's hesitation, just enough for everyone in the room to remark on it. "I do believe I had planned a short trip into the village for tomorrow. Perhaps another day." As Maman looked at her in horror at this unheard of breach of manners, Kitty belatedly realized that a ride would be the best way to extract information or find out something about Montfort's habits. "On second thought, I'd be delighted to ride tomorrow," she blurted out, then felt herself blush as everyone looked at her with raised eyebrows. "I forgot the day that I was supposed to visit a friend," she amended lamely. It sounded false even to her ears.

"Excellent," said Montfort smoothly. "I'll meet you at

the stables early tomorrow morning. You can, I'm sure, show me the best places to ride along the beach." With that, he returned to his conversation with Kitty's mother, while Kitty collapsed rather gracelessly into a nearby chair. Thomas sat across from her and stared at her curiously.

Supper went no better for Kitty. She sat in silence while Montfort regaled the family with tales of his adventures in France. Kitty did notice that he was very careful of her mother's sensibilities and did not in any way disparage the French. For that, she was thankful and did think a little better of him. No one knew what slights her mother had endured from some of the *ton*. It was one of the reasons Sir Jerome had removed his family to Bellevoir to stay. Montfort also skirted the stories being told of carnage and hardship, instead concentrating his tales on charming reminiscences of places and people he had seen. Kitty could see that he had quite captivated her mother.

Finally, they adjourned to the drawing room, where Montfort declared himself no good at cards, but did ask if Kitty could entertain them at the pianoforte with a song. Thomas broke out in laughter at this suggestion, and was unkind enough to tell Montfort that if he'd ever heard Kit sing, he would never put forth such an idea. To cover the breach, Maman and Thomas had to sing some French ditties and play for them. Kitty chalked down another black mark against Thomas in her mental ledger. He was going to pay for all these insults someday, and, she promised herself, it would be soon.

Maman came back to her seat after her songs. She did have a beautiful voice, which, unfortunately, she had bequeathed to Thomas rather than to Kitty. "Now, Captain Montfort, you must tell us of your plans," she said, sitting down across from the visitor.

"Are you going to stay at Sherbourne or do you plan to return to London for the season?"

"I plan to return to London for a short while," he answered, "but not until late in the season. I've been quite busy repairing and redecorating Sherbourne. In many ways, that task has been more demanding than a military campaign," he said with a smile, "but now I have everything almost ready."

"Ready?" Kitty asked. "Ready for what?"

He gave her an amused glance that reminded her of Thomas. "I plan to ask my cousin to come spend some time with me. Perhaps you know her from your stay in London. Miss Marianne Montfort."

Kitty thought. "I don't recall meeting her, but then I was in London only a short while. I prefer to stay here at Bellevoir."

"I can see why. Such a charming place." He paused. "I hope you'll be able to visit my cousin. She isn't acquainted with anyone in the neighborhood, and I don't wish her to be lonely."

"It will be a change from London," Kitty agreed perfunctorily, mainly to make conversation.

"Yes, it will. I've asked a friend of mine to accompany Marianne and keep her company for a while. You must come over and help them plan entertainments. I believe you're quite well acquainted with my cousin's, ah, friend, Miss Harriette Marlowe."

Kitty could hear Thomas chuckle in the background as she tried hard to keep a straight face. "Miss Marlowe and I have met," she said shortly.

"Wonderful," said Montfort. "When I wrote and asked her to come to Sherbourne and stay a few weeks with Marianne, I mentioned that you lived nearby. Harriette informed me that the two of you were the closest of friends."

Kitty almost choked. Close friends! Kitty loathed

the ground Harriette Marlowe walked on, and Harriette knew it. And Montfort had had the nerve to call her *Harriette!* They must be practically betrothed. After carefully making her face blank, she glanced over at Thomas to see how he was taking this news. Kitty found he was, from the fatuous grin on his face, enjoying it immensely. He was even chuckling again.

Montfort glanced at Thomas with a puzzled look, then turned again to Kitty. "Perhaps I might bring Marianne and Miss Marlowe over for a short visit one day soon. They're due to arrive at Sherbourne on the day after tomorrow."

"By all means, Captain." Lord Walsingham entered the conversation. "I'm quite sure Catherine would enjoy seeing her friend again, and I know she would be delighted to make the acquaintance of your cousin."

Thomas was unable to keep the laughter out of his voice. "Oh, yes. Kitty will be on tenterhooks until she sees Miss Marlowe again, I'm sure. Isn't that right, Kit?"

Kitty forced a smile. "You've no idea of my feelings for Miss Marlowe," she said through her teeth.

"Splendid," Montfort said, rising to leave. "I shall meet you tomorrow morning for a ride, Miss Walsingham, and we can discuss some entertainments for Marianne and Har . . . Miss Marlowe." Montfort bowed and took his leave.

Kitty stalked up the stairs to her chamber, followed by Thomas who mimicked her in a high falsetto, "You've no idea of my feelings for Miss Marlowe." He started to say it again, but had to stop as he doubled up with laughter. Kitty glared at him and slammed the door to her chamber. Thomas was still laughing as he went down the hall.

Chapter Four

Kitty awoke the next morning with the early sun shining on her face. Dimly she heard her name being called. "Kit, where the devil are you." Drowsily, she recognized the voice as belonging to Thomas and started to get up to answer. Aches and pains stopped her, and she realized she was sitting cramped in the damask chair in the library with only a coverlet wrapped over her night clothes.

"Here you are," he said irritably, crossing the library floor in quick strides. "What in the world are you doing down in the library at this time of the morning? Don't you know that Montfort's been waiting for you in the parlor for above a half an hour?"

"Ooohh." Kitty wasn't sure if the wail was because she had forgotten about Montfort's invitation to ride or because her cold and cramped feet protested at being placed on the carpet.

Thomas took another look at her. "Good God, Kit! Look how you're dressed!" He looked again. "Or rather undressed," he amended. "Don't tell me you spent the night here in a chair. Whatever for?"

Kitty stared at him, trying to look assured. "I came downstairs to watch for the smugglers, Thomas. *You* evidently don't intend to assist me, so I felt I had to do it myself." She tried to stand regally, but her numb feet refused to support her, and she fell backwards into the chair.

"Of all the harebrained, crack-brained, feather-headed . . ." Thomas ran out of vivid words and just stood staring at her. "You defy description, Kit."

Kitty opened her mouth to reply, but then in total horror, she heard the library door open and Montfort's voice. "Have you located my riding partner, Thomas?" His tone was definitely amused.

Montfort strolled over to the chair, impeccably garbed in buckskins and a riding coat of dark brown trimmed in almond, his chestnut hair glinting gold in the sun from the window. With a single glance he measured Kitty from her bare feet, up over the coverlet she clasped to her to cover her nightrail, to her undressed hair. "Sleeping late, Miss Walsingham?"

"I, uh, I could not sleep last night and came down to locate a new novel, and fell asleep in the library." It was quite obviously a lie, but Montfort was too much the gentleman to question it. After all, it was plausible.

"I quite understand." His eyes raked her again, this time accompanied by a smile that quite smacked of a leer. "Perhaps we should postpone our ride until another time. If you wished to wait until tomorrow, Marianne and Miss Marlowe might join us if they have rested suitably from their journey."

"No!" Kitty yelped, sitting up so quickly that the coverlet slipped down and exposed the top of her laced and beribboned nightrail. As Montfort raised an expressive eyebrow, she snatched the coverlet and raised it to her chin. "That is, I should like to ride today, if you don't mind. After spending the night here in a chair, I, uh, feel the need to get out in the fresh air."

"As you wish, Miss Walsingham, although I suggest we wait until this afternoon so that you might, ah, don more suitable attire." Montfort tried but he was unable to keep the chuckle out of his voice. Kitty was sure he was going to break into full laughter at any moment.

"I'd have to agree with Montfort," Thomas chimed in. "You can't very well go rattling around the country on a horse while you're dressed in nothing but a nightrail. I tell you, Kitty, it just ain't done."

Kitty turned and unleashed her frustrations and embarrassment on Thomas. "I *know* that, you idiot! Do you think I planned to go riding in my *nightclothes*? Furthermore, I can't imagine what kind of gentleman would even *think* such a thing." She stopped and glared at Montfort. "Also, I can't imagine what kind of gentleman would stand around the library while a lady is . . . is . . ." She stopped, groping for the right word.

Montfort supplied it. "En deshaibille?"

Thomas stared at her before her meaning hit him. "Montfort, that's it—deshaibille." He peered at Kitty, not mistaking her glare this time. "I do think Kit wants us to leave so she can get out of that demmed coverlet and go get dressed."

"I do believe you're right, Thomas," Montfort said. The voice was smooth, but his eyes never left Kitty. She could have sworn that he could see right through the coverlet and her thin nightrail. Not only that, but he was actually laughing at her. Not laughing aloud, but she could see the laughter in his eyes and there was that tell-tale quirk at the corner of his mouth. "Perhaps, Miss Walsingham, since you're determined to go today, we should plan to ride later in the morning, say, in two hours. Will that give you time to dress and breakfast?" He chuckled as he spoke.

"Of course it will," Kitty snapped.

As the library door closed behind Thomas and Montfort, she could hear them break out into laughter. It was beyond humiliating. She wrapped the coverlet around her and fled to her chamber, hoping no one would see her hopping and hobbling up the stairs on her cramped legs and feet. It could have been worse, she reminded herself as she staggered uncertainly down the hall to her room, dragging the coverlet behind her. Montfort could have had Harriette Marlowe with him to see her humiliation. It was small comfort.

By midmorning, Kitty had breakfasted and dressed in her old riding habit of forest green. Bidwell had done everything possible to coax her into the fashionable new gray one, but Kit would not be persuaded. She knew the old habit was worn and quite out of fashion, but some perverse notion would not let her go out preening in front of Montfort. Especially not after the morning's humiliation. Bidwell gave in after much protest, but still muttered the whole time Kitty dressed. Bidwell consoled herself by dressing Kitty's hair in an especially becoming mass of curls around her face, then tucking a new feather into her hat.

Kitty came downstairs and went to the stables, only to find Montfort already waiting for her, standing by his big black stallion, giving Thomas pointers about looking for the best in horseflesh. Thomas was standing there, avidly drinking in every word. Kitty had to chuckle to herself, knowing that Thomas probably knew or cared less than anyone in the house about horses.

She ventured to tell Montfort as much as they rode out of the yard towards the rolling fields that led to the cliffs by the sea. "Do you mean my fine lesson was wasted?" he asked.

"I'm afraid so. If you had been able to discourse on the relative merits of the latest fashions in waistcoats, then Thomas might know what you were talking about. I regret to tell you, but horses are quite beyond his ken."

Montfort shook his head and smiled at her. He had a very nice smile, she noticed absently. "And I thought all the Walsinghams were bruising riders."

"Not Thomas," she said with an answering smile. "Thomas has his good points, but riding isn't one of them." She pulled up her horse at the edge of the field. "I believe they've had enough of a warmup. Would you like to race to the sea?"

He looked at her quizzically. "Do you wish a head start?"

"Of course not! You're not talking to Thomas. My Beau may not have the power of your horse, Captain Montfort, but I assure you that he's as fast as the wind."

"We shall see," he said with a laugh, and in a moment they were away across the field, leaving the grooms far behind. Kitty was delighted to be again on the back of her horse, flying across the ground with the smell of the sea on the air. She could hear Montfort's big black beside her, rapidly moving ahead, hooves pounding into the soft sandy ground. Beau was as fast as the wind, but the big black had longer, more powerful legs, and passed ahead just as the field gave way to the sandy grass that signalled the beginning of the beach. Kitty pulled her horse up to slow him and cantered up to where Montfort waited.

"Well done, Captain Montfort." Not only his horse, but also his riding had been superb, and Kit was fair enough to acknowledge a bruising rider when she met one.

He nodded his head in acknowledgement. "And the same to you, Miss Walsingham. I can see that you indeed have the famous Walsingham way with horses." He glanced down at Beau. "And I also commend your horse. He has great spirit."

Kitty reached down and stroked the gelding's neck with affection. "Beau and I have been together for a while. We understand each other."

"Really?" His eyebrow quirked. "His name is Beau?"

Kitty nodded. "He was a gift from my grandmère when I was fourteen. Because of her, I wanted to give him a French name, and, since we became such good friends immediately, it seemed to suit him." They turned the horses and slowly began riding down the beach.

"I had heard your family had strong French connections," Montfort remarked.

There was silence for a moment as Kitty waited for him to say something else. Finally she spoke. "Yes, I think everyone in England knows about my mother and her family."

There was a short silence, as though he were searching for something to say. "Did you enjoy your recent trip to France?"

"Yes." Kitty glanced at him, but saw nothing in his face to indicate anything other than idle questioning. "I went over to spend some time with my grandmother."

There was another stretch of silence. Kitty thought to herself that as a spy, she certainly wasn't very good at eliciting information. And unfortunately, Captain Montfort wasn't volunteering anything. She tried again. "I enjoyed hearing about your adventures in France. Did you like the countryside?"

His voice was quiet. "Yes, very much. I liked many of the French people I met in the country. Many of them, of course, were devoted to Bonaparte, but that was to be expected. I found much kindness, especially after I was wounded." There was an odd note, almost a bitterness, to his voice.

"I noticed you didn't mention your injury last night. It must have been very difficult for you."

He glanced at her again, trying to read her expression. "I prefer not to mention it if at all possible. That experience is past and is no longer of great consequence."

"Was it bad for you?" Kitty sensed he was hiding his feelings and felt compassion for him.

He reined up his horse and sat looking at the waves breaking on a spit of land stretching out into the Channel. "Not as bad for me as for some of my friends," he said at last, quietly.

"You had friends with you?"

He turned and looked at her, his emotion visible for a moment, but then he carefully shuttered his face. "I called them my friends, and truly they were. Most of the men under my command suffered greatly. We were pinned down against a small ridge." There was a long pause while Montfort dealt with his memories. "I regret to say there were heavy casualties."

Kitty licked her lips and paused. Thomas would have castigated her curiosity, but she had to know. "And you, how did you escape?"

The bitterness in his voice came out again. "I was hit in the back and tried to command from a litter. As the French closed in, my men carried me out to safety. Unfortunately, most of them sacrificed themselves. There were only ten of us left by the time we reached the field hospital."

"I'm very sorry." There seemed nothing else to say.

Suddenly, he composed himself, turned, and flashed a smile at her. "The fortunes of war, Miss Walsingham. Every soldier knows that and accepts it as a part of his credo and his fate." He turned his horse. "Now, we shall ride down the beach and you shall tell me of every nook and cranny in the shoreline. I hear there are some fascinating stories circulating about pirates and smugglers."

"Smugglers?" Kitty could not believe her ears. Here she had been thinking of a way to broach the subject, and now Captain Montfort was *asking* her about possible places for a smuggler to hide. She tried to gather her wits about her. "I'm sure there are many stories and many spots for smugglers to hide. Have you investigated the shoreline at Sherbourne?"

"Oh, indeed I have, Miss Walsingham. You may be sure it was one of the first things I asked about when I was considering the property."

Kitty felt her eyes widen. The man was not only bringing up the question of smugglers, he was practically *confessing!* "You know about the smuggling around here?" She was aghast. Then she caught herself up. No proper spy would express such emotion. "That is, I mean, you've heard all the stories about smuggling here on the coast?"

He smiled at her. "Rumors in London but otherwise, only what the locals have hinted. I had very much hoped you might enlighten me, Miss Walsingham." His eyes suddenly seemed to be assessing her. "You've heard all the stories, I assume."

Kitty stiffened. "Oh, yes, but then everyone has heard gossip. That's all it is, I'm sure — gossip. You know how everyone in a small place knows everything about everyone else."

His smile was back. "Ah yes, I know, and I thought you just might be the person who knew about everyone and everything around here and would have the time to tell me all about it."

"I?" Kitty felt suddenly out of her depth. "You think I gather and disseminate all the local gossip? I assure you, Captain, that you probably know more about what goes on around here than I do. Besides, Captain, you forget that I've been gone for several weeks. I'm hardly acquainted with the latest in local gossip."

His tone was soothing. "Not gossip, Miss Walsingham. I merely thought you might have some entertaining stories to share about it."

"It?"

"The smuggling, Miss Walsingham. Surely, as a local, you know all about it." There was a short pause. "You might even have heard some of the stories about people around here assisting the French." He hesitated a moment. "Perhaps you have even heard some stories about Napoleon himself."

Anger suddenly welled up in Kitty. "That's it, isn't it? You think that because we have French relations that we're doing everything possible to help Bonaparte." She felt an overwhelming white rage. "You're despicable!" With that, she wheeled her horse and fled toward Bellevoir, leaving Montfort and his big black standing on the shore.

"Now, Kit, you're probably blowing this thing all up," Thomas said to her. He had found her in the library, alternating between angry pacing and angry tears. "Montfort's a right sort. I'm sure he didn't mean what you thought. You're thinking the worst here, and you know how you are to jump to conclusions sometimes." He stopped as Kitty muttered angrily, then continued. "Anyhow, it was a little much, you labeling him despicable. Not *ton*, you know."

"Then why would he ask such a thing?" she shot back.

Thomas draped himself languidly over the damask sofa. "Probably just making conversation. Or maybe he's just a Londoner looking for some excitement with the smugglers. Who knows?"

Kitty resumed her pacing. "Then you admit that he's involved in the smuggling," she said triumphantly.

"I didn't say that, Kit. You're doing it again—jumping to conclusions and never listening. I said the man was probably just curious. You should know all about curiosity." He smiled at her.

"Quit changing the subject, Thomas."

"Kit, be reasonable. You can't make charges like this until you have some proof, and I for one don't think a war hero like Montfort would dream of dabbling in a few contraband silks and satins. Rumor says he's more than well fixed—something over twenty thousand a year at least."

"Maybe he gambled it away and needs the money. He looks like a gamester if I've ever seen one."

Thomas groaned and got up. "For God's sake, Kit. Quit being gothic. I'm going to talk to Papa right now and see about burning all those novels you read. They're turning your mind to mush." With that he stalked out before Kitty could reply.

"Novels, indeed," she said to a closed door. "Just wait, Thomas Walsingham. I know something is going on here, and I intend to get to the bottom of it. If you want proof, then that's exactly what I'll get for you. You and everyone around here shall have your proof."

Chapter Five

Kitty slept badly that night. Over and over she played out the scene with Montfort in her mind. She could find only one possible explanation for his questions. And he had been questioning her about the French sympathies of her family, Kitty was sure of it, no matter what Thomas thought. The only reason Montfort could have been asking such questions was to enlist Kitty and her family in his schemes. Perhaps he planned to use the shore at Bellevoir as a base to avoid suspicion at Sherbourne. Perhaps he even wanted the Walsinghams to help him with his smuggling. Kitty arose and paced the floor impatiently. Such a suggestion was hardly to be borne, but that had to be the answer. Nothing else fit.

And she had thrown away the chance to find out anything about his plans. She must have proof of her suspicions, and to do that, she had to discover what he was up to. She thought of and discarded a dozen possibilities. If it weren't the smuggling, he might even be a spy for the French. What better cover could he have than that of a wounded war hero, conveniently situated and recuperating on the coast where messages could be sent quickly across the Channel?

She went over and looked out her chamber window to see only the blackness that lay between Bellevoir and the Channel. She had to expose Montfort, but to do that, she had to have proof for Thomas, for her father, and for the authorities. That was the key to putting away a traitor like Montfort. But to prove him a Judas to England, she must be on friendly terms with him. There was no other way.

But, she decided quickly as she paced around the floor again, there would be no apology on her part. She would never do it. That left only one avenue— Thomas. She would simply have to convince Thomas to placate the man, a job Thomas could handle admirably. She climbed the three steps beside her high canopied bed, and sat perched on the edge of the mattress. The job of getting Thomas to erase the afternoon's quarrel with Montfort would be delicate. As dunderheaded as Thomas was, he might even tell the man about Kitty's suspicions. No, this was going to take management, but Kitty was sure she could manage Thomas quite well. With a smile, she curled up under the covers and dozed off.

Kitty slept until around nine and then got up, knowing she would have to wait until Thomas got up at his usual hour of ten or eleven. To her amazement, she learned that Thomas had risen early and ridden out, no one knew where. For Thomas to ride anywhere at all was surprising in itself, but for him to get up early to do so was cause for complete wonderment. Kitty was on tenterhooks until the afternoon when she heard him coming in the yard. She snatched up a book and curled up in one of the red chairs in the library, feigning ennui.

"Reading, Kit?" Thomas asked as he walked over to the desk and, from a lower drawer, removed a large piece of parchment that looked suspiciously like a map.

"Yes, a most boring novel," Kitty answered, straining her eyes to see the paper in his hand. She could have sworn he was trying to hide it.

He glanced at her and made a face. "Might be a bit easier for you to read if you turned it right side up," he said dryly, walking out of the library, parchment in hand, closing the door behind him.

Kitty gave up all pretense and wrenched open the library door. "Thomas, you wait right there! I want to talk to you."

"Sorry, Kit, I can't spare the time right now. I'm in something of a rush." She heard Duff close the door behind him as he called the groom to bring his horse. She flew to the front door in time to see him riding away, gamely balancing himself in the saddle and holding on for dear life.

"Now just where was he going?" she asked of no one in particular as she stood in the door.

There was a wheeze behind her as Duff, the butler, waited patiently for her to get out of the way. "I believe the young master was going to Sherbourne," he gasped between wheezes.

"Sherbourne! Did he say why?" Kitty was aghast.

Duff pushed the door shut a few more inches, his wispy white hair blowing in the breeze. "The young master did not confide the nature of his journey."

Taking this for the proper set-down it was, Kitty mumbled a thank you to Duff and removed herself from the door. It annoyed her that Duff still seemed to think she and Thomas were in leading strings, but then Duff and his father before him had been with Papa's family for an eternity. Duff seemed to think she was incapable of thought.

With Thomas's mission a mystery, Kitty sped back to the library and began searching the desk drawer for a clue to the parchment Thomas had removed. It had been a map, Kit was sure of that much, and it looked like an old one. Thomas was taking a map of something to Sherbourne. Had Montfort somehow duped poor Thomas into being an accomplice to his schemes? It was entirely possible.

Kitty dismissed the idea of going to her father with her story—he would demand proof and she didn't have any. Besides, there was no way she was going to implicate Thomas in anything. There was nothing for it except to wait until Thomas returned from wherever he had gone and then confront him.

By late afternoon, Kitty had paced the floor for what seemed like miles, given up on reading, and tossed her needlework aside after tangling her threads hopelessly. Even a short ride on Beau had not livened her spirits. Her ride seemed to take her to the boundaries of Sherbourne, but she could see nothing. She thought about riding boldly up to the door on some pretext, but she was certainly not audacious enough to flaunt propriety so. It seemed all she could do was wait, and everyone, including Kitty herself, knew she was not good at waiting.

A rattle of carriage wheels roused Kitty from the fidgets. She dashed to the door and waited impatiently while the knocker boomed, and Duff wheezed and shuffled his way into opening the door.

"Richard?"

He stood amidst his luggage and stared at her. "Not a very warm welcome, Kitty. And here Thomas assured me you'd welcome me with open arms." He sounded aggrieved.

"Richard?" Kitty seemed incapable of speech.

"Yes, Richard. Lord, you know who I am, Kit." He paused and looked at her. "What's the matter, Kit? Is my waistcoat covered with soup or have I aged beyond recognition since I saw you last?" He took a step toward her.

"Richard!" she cried in welcome, clasping his arm.

"Do come in and forgive my ragtag manners. I was never so glad to see anyone before!"

Gratified, he stepped over his portmanteaux and motioned to his man to attend to them. "That's a relief, Kitty. I was beginning to think I was going to have to turn around and head back to London tonight. Thomas wrote and promised me that . . . "

Kitty stopped short. "Thomas wrote you?"

He laughed. "Still the same impulsive Kitty, aren't you?" As she blushed, he continued. "Yes, Thomas wrote and told me you were back from France. He invited me down for two or three weeks before he and I go up to Scotland for some hunting." He stood back and regarded her critically. "After seeing you in such high bloom, I'm certainly glad I decided to come to Bellevoir. I don't know which, but either France or your time here rusticating on the coast has done wonders for you."

Kitty looked up at him and grinned. "Am I to understand then that I seemed an invalid while in London and now appear to have recovered?"

Richard groaned and ran his fingers through his tousled Brutus cut. "Lord, Kit. I've done it again." He looked down into her laughing face. "Every time I try to come up with a compliment for you, I seem to put not one, but both feet, squarely in my mouth. Please tell me I'm forgiven. What I meant to say was . . ." He paused, fumbling for the words while Kitty waited, smiling. "Dash it all, Kit. I'm trying to tell you how good you look!"

"Compliment accepted, Richard," she said with a laugh as she propelled him into the library and rang for tea. "Sit down and tell me all the *on dits*. Much as I love Bellevoir, it's still good to hear all the London gossip." She watched as Richard arranged his tall frame on the sofa across from her. He looked much the same as he had last time she had seen him—Richard was always the same. He was tall, almost six feet, but not thin. Richard had been stocky since childhood, and in time, he would be as heavy as his father. He had the Collingwood coloring—curly ginger hair, bright blue eyes, and fair skin. Richard had the Collingwood disposition as well—he was always calm and cheerful. Kitty had taken shameless advantage of those traits since they were in leading strings. She had been able to talk Richard into doing anything for her. It occurred to her that she might still be able to do so. Yes, she thought to herself, it might be quite fortuitous that Richard was here to help her now.

"Not much happening right now in town," he said, taking a cup of tea and a biscuit from her. "London's a dead place, so I hear. I haven't been in town much lately as I've been spending most of my time remodeling the farm. I don't really know, but I've heard that almost everyone's either in the country or gone to Paris. With Boney put away, it's the first time anyone's felt like going abroad. More English in Paris right now than Parisians, so they say."

"What a pity. I was looking forward to some scintillating gossip. I haven't heard anything since before I left for France. Thomas knows everything, but he won't tell me."

"Why not?" Richard reached for another biscuit while Kitty refilled his teacup.

Kitty gave a sound distinctly like a snort. "He 'doesn't want to sully my ears with lowlife gossip.' And that's a direct quote."

Richard laughed aloud. "What Thomas is afraid of is that he'll have to admit to his part in some of the goings-on. If I know you, Kitty, you'd not be above resorting to blackmail."

"You do me an injustice, Richard. I merely wanted

to hear what the *ton* was doing."

Richard reached for a third biscuit. "As I said, not much. I did hear that Harriette Marlowe had snagged a live 'un. Haven't seen any announcements, though." He wrinkled his brow. "I believe it was Sobey's brother. He's in the army, I think. Would have thought Harriette wouldn't have settled for less than an earl, but then, somebody told me it was a love match. Although I also heard that Harriette's mother was promoting it because Sobey's brother, Montwick or something like that, had an income of at least fifty thousand a year."

"His name's Captain Montfort, and Thomas told me it was twenty thousand a year," Kitty said as she poured yet another cup of tea for Richard. "And as for Harriette Marlowe ever being involved in a love match . . . never. The woman has a head full of schemes, not a heart full of romance."

Richard looked insulted. "Well, Kit, you should have told me you already knew all this."

"I didn't know. I still don't know."

"Sounds as if you're up on Miss Marlowe's doings. As I remember, she ain't one of your favorite people." Richard looked at her over the edge of his teacup.

"Bosh! I have absolutely no interest at all in anything Harriette Marlowe does. My only interest stems from the fact that Montfort happens to have bought Sherbourne and moved in next door. Thomas is quite taken with him."

Richard sat up. "Bought Sherbourne? I didn't know old Tillbury would ever sell. I would have gone after it myself. A prime piece of property, and right here on the coast."

"That brings up something I wanted to talk to you about, Richard," Kitty began smoothly.

"Do you know how much he gave for it?"

"Whatever are you talking about, Richard?"

He gave her an aggrieved look. "I'm talking about Sherbourne, what else, Kit? I've had my eye on that property for years, and now some captain who's rich as Croesus comes back from the wars and buys it right out from under my nose. I'd wager he bought all five hundred acres of it, too. Damme!" Richard put his teacup down hard on the tray and sloshed tea all over. "Sorry," he mumbled, reaching for a napkin. "Do you think he'd sell it, Kit?"

"You'll have to ask him yourself, Richard. Captain Montfort and I don't happen to be that close. Now, there's something I'd like to discuss with you."

He smiled at her. "Of course, Kit. I'm all yours."

There was a commotion in the hall, and then the library door was flung open without ceremony. "Richard!" Thomas burst in and greeted his friend while Kitty sat back in resignation. Her discussion with Richard would have to wait until she could get him alone. She certainly couldn't ask him for his help in unraveling the smuggling plot until Thomas was out of the way.

"Has Kitty been entertaining you?" Thomas asked, helping himself to a cup of tea and a biscuit.

"Oh, yes. Welcomed me with open arms, just like you said she would."

Thomas had the grace to look sheepish. "Did you think me completely lacking in manners, brother?" Kit asked him.

Thomas took a bite of his biscuit and glanced at his sister. "Manners? With you, Kit, I never know. I seem to recall a time or two when you've skirted the edge." He looked knowingly at her.

"Thomas, why didn't you tell me Sherbourne was for sale?" Richard asked. "I'd have been interested in it myself. Kitty's been telling me that Sobey's brother bought it."

"Captain Montfort. A capital fellow, just back from the wars. You should see him with the ribbons, Richard. As a matter of fact, I think you might have been with me when we watched him race with Francis Brentwood on the Bristol Road."

"Not me." Richard was still thinking about Sherbourne. "Do you think he might sell the place? I hear that he's well off, something like fifty thousand a year. Besides, I heard Sobey had given him the town house in London. What would a man with fifty thousand and a town house want with a place on the coast anyway?"

"My point exactly," Kitty said.

"Now, Kit," Thomas warned. Turning to Richard, he explained, "Kitty's got some kind of maggoty notion in her head that Montfort's involved in the local smuggling. Too many of those trashy novels is what I think. The poor girl has turned her mind to mush. Can you just imagine, Richard, a war hero like Captain Montfort involved in smuggling a bale of silk and a few bottles of champagne!"

"Laugh if you wish, Thomas. You must admit that certain events have been quite suspicious." Kitty glared at him. "Besides, I believe more happens to be at stake than a bale of silk and some bottles of champagne."

Richard lifted an eyebrow at her. "What do you mean by that, Kitty?"

Before Kitty could speak, Thomas interrupted. "What Kitty means is that she has nothing to do with her life except spin fairy tales. What she needs is a household to manage and a nursery full of brats just as addle-pated as she is."

"Speak for yourself, Thomas," Kitty snapped. "At least I do more with my time than spend my whole life watching some dandy of the *ton* race up and down the Bristol Road. There's more to life than the perfect waistcoat."

Richard stood. "You two never change. Still arguing like a pair of five year olds." He smiled from one to the other. "And it's a strange thing, but you're still arguing over much the same thing you did when you were five."

"Hardly," Kitty sniffed. "By the way, Thomas, why don't you tell us where you've been and what you've been doing all day."

"Nothing much." He rolled his eyes at Richard. "See, she's turning into a regular shrew. Next thing I know, she'll have *me* involved in smuggling. Perhaps even Montfort and myself piloting the boat under cover of moonlight, seeking a safe haven for our nefarious goings-on. If you stay long, Richard, she'll have you in with us."

Richard laughed. "Not me. I'm much too commonplace to be involved in anything except farming. I would like to find my chamber and change before dinner, though."

"Kit's probably got you staying out in the henhouse so you can spy on Sherbourne for her," Thomas said, only half in jest.

Kitty sprang to her feet. "How little you think of me, Thomas. I did tell Duff to have a room prepared for Richard and had him call a footman to take the portmanteaux up. I'm not all that scatterbrained, you know."

"Merely teasing, Kit," Thomas said, mending his fences. "Come on, Richard. We have several things to talk about before dinner, and I'm sure Kit needs some time to herself." Thomas guided Richard out of the library, and Kitty heard them going up the stairs, laughing and talking as old friends do.

Maman came in to find Kitty still sitting. "Did I hear voices? I thought you might have been entertaining someone."

"Richard has come to spend some time with us," Kitty answered.

"Ah, oui. Thomas asked if he could invite Richard down to stay a while and, of course, it was all right." She smiled down at Kitty. "Thomas had already written and asked him down, so it was after the fact, but Richard has always been welcome here."

"Did Thomas ask him down for a reason, Maman?"

Her mother laughed. "Ah, I believe you've already seen through Thomas's grand plan. And he thought he was being so subtle."

"Thomas? Subtle? It was more than obvious, Maman. Thomas was talking about managing households and filling up nurseries," Kitty said ruefully.

Maman laughed again and gave Kitty a quick hug. "You must do what you feel best whenever you feel the time is right. Now the time is right to dress for dinner, n'est-ce pas?" With another smile, she left.

Kit sat for a moment, thinking over the things Thomas had dropped during his conversation with Richard. She had also noted that Thomas had dodged her question about his whereabouts during the day.

"It has to be," she said to herself with more than a little astonishment. "Thomas has to know what Montfort is doing, else why would he keep trying to throw me off the track? Nurseries, indeed!"

With that cheering thought, she went up to dress for dinner.

Chapter Six

The next morning Kitty was up early and had a cup of chocolate in bed as Bidwell fussed around and finally selected a bright yellow morning gown trimmed with braided yellow and white ribands.

"You'll want ribands in your hair, of course," she said, holding up two to see which matched the dress.

"Why all the fuss, Bidwell?" Kitty asked. "I can manage perfectly well with my buff gown and no ribands."

Bidwell gave her a disgusted look which spoke volumes. "I'm certain you could manage quite well in that gown, but you know you look washed out in buff. I'm sure Lord Richard would prefer seeing you in this yellow."

Kitty laughed. "Bidwell, you of all people have been here long enough to know that Richard has seen me in every state from leading strings to a covering of mud, and it hasn't made any difference."

Bidwell sniffed. "Yes, but that was when you were a child. Things have changed since then. Now, believe me, you're of an age when you can catch more flies with honey."

Kitty sat up on the edge of the bed and put her chocolate down. "Bidwell, you amaze me. Have you and your colleagues belowstairs decided that I'm out to catch Lord Richard?"

Bidwell didn't deign to answer; she merely maneuvered Kitty so that she could hold the yellow and the ribands up to her hair. "Very good," she said.

Kitty, from enduring long years of Bidwell's stubbornness, knew better than to argue. After all, Bidwell was right—the yellow did look very good on her. She put on the dress and sat quietly as Bidwell dressed her hair, braiding the ribands into it.

Richard was already at breakfast whenever she went down. He looked up with a smile when she entered. "I say, Kitty, you're looking very fine this morning."

"Thank you, Richard. You're looking splendid yourself." It was quite true. Richard was dressed in riding clothes, a garb which became him. "I hope you're not planning on taking Thomas for a ride. His seat hasn't improved a whit, I'm sorry to say."

Richard laughed. "I learned long ago that a ride with Thomas was an experience not to be repeated. No, what I had in mind was asking you if you'd like to go riding with me and show me around."

Kitty's face was puzzled. "You've seen Bellevoir a dozen times, Richard. Nothing at all has changed."

"That was merely an excuse, Kitty. I wanted to ask you to go riding with me." His face was suffused with red. Kitty had forgotten how easily Richard blushed when he was embarrassed.

"But of course, Richard. All you had to do was ask. I've been trying to take Beau out regularly for the past few days anyway. He needs the exercise."

Richard's face resumed its normal hue. "That's capital. Right after breakfast?" He began to fill his plate from the array of food on the sideboard. "Muffins, Kitty?" He handed her a plate with one.

Kitty watched in fascination as Richard ate an enormous breakfast while she nibbled on a muffin and drank another cup of chocolate. Richard's father, had become obese of late, and Kitty feared that Richard was on the same path. She was toying with the idea of suggesting a diet when Thomas came into the room. He poured a cup of tea and sat down.

"Would you like to go with me to Portsmouth today, Richard?" he asked.

Richard finished a mouthful of grilled kidneys. "Kitty and I were going out riding, but if you wish me to go, I'm sure Kitty won't mind postponing our ride."

"Riding, well, that's good. Not wasting any time, are you, Kit?" Thomas looked from Kitty to Richard in a way that made her distinctly uncomfortable. She knew exactly what he was thinking.

"I'm sure your trip to Portsmouth would be more entertaining for Richard," she said. "Why are you going?"

Thomas looked quickly down into his cup, and Kitty knew immediately that he was going to tell her a lie. Thomas was really one of the most abominable liars she knew. "Going to visit a friend," he mumbled into his cup.

"Really? Who is it? Someone I know?"

"No, just an . . ." Thomas tried to look her in the eyes, but instead managed to study the carvings on the sideboard carefully. "Just an old school friend."

"I don't remember anybody from school who lives in Portsmouth," Richard said, oblivious to Thomas's difficulty.

"A friend of a friend, really," Thomas said. "No one you know, I'm sure, so you really don't have to feel obligated to go. You and Kitty go ahead with your ride."

"Wouldn't hear of it," Richard said. "Kitty and I can go riding any time. Do you plan on riding to

Portsmouth?"

"Good God, no!" Thomas was close to being horrified. "We'll take the carriage." Thomas rose and headed for the door. "I wouldn't dream of riding to Portsmouth when I can ride in a nice civilized carriage. I'll meet you out front in half an hour."

Richard stood to follow. "Richard, a moment," Kitty said. She paused briefly, not quite sure how to begin as he sat back down next to her. "Richard, do you remember what Thomas said about Montfort yesterday?" At Richard's nod, she continued. "Montfort has been making up to Thomas, and I'm sure this trip to Portsmouth has something to do with Montfort in some way."

"Now, Kitty . . . ," Richard began. "Thomas told me last night that . . ."

"Hush, Richard," Kitty broke in. "Thomas is the very worst liar in the world, and he was lying just now. He doesn't have any friend of a friend in Portsmouth, and I know it. I want you to go along and tell me about this 'friend' he's supposed to meet."

"Kitty, I couldn't do that. Thomas and I are friends." Richard looked appalled. "He wouldn't want me carrying tales, and I wouldn't want to do it. It just ain't done, you know."

"Don't think of it as carrying tales, Richard. Think of it as saving Thomas from himself. If he's involved in something shady with Montfort, it's our duty to rescue him."

Richard looked doubtful. "Thomas can usually get himself out of any scrapes he gets into. I don't care much for being a spy."

Kitty moved closer to him. "Richard, you wouldn't be spying, you would be helping Thomas. You would be helping me." She paused and looked at him with what she hoped was an anxious expression. "You don't know how worried I've been about Thomas," she said, hoping Richard wouldn't know she was lying as well. "It would be such a help if you could watch him today and tell me what he does."

"Well, since you put it that way . . ." Richard looked doubtfully at her, still not completely convinced. "I'll tell you what he does, but only within reason."

"Good!" Kitty felt quite victorious. "Now you'd better hurry. Thomas will be ready to leave in a few minutes." With that, she almost pushed him out the breakfast room door.

The day dragged on while she waited for Thomas and Richard to return. Kitty tried a dozen things to pass the time during the morning. The afternoon was much better—she sat with Maman and read aloud to her while Maman did her exquisite needlework. Finally, just after dark she heard the carriage wheels, but there was no time to quiz Richard. Kitty reached the door in time to hear Duff inform both Thomas and Richard that there was to be an early supper which would be served in half an hour. She stood there as Thomas rushed by her with a wink and Richard with an apologetic grin.

"Damme!" she muttered, to Duff's horror.

At supper, Thomas was in high spirits, and Kitty couldn't wait to get Richard aside and talk to him. There was no opportunity until well after supper when they all gathered in the drawing room. She finally maneuvered Richard over toward the corner of the room. "What happened today?" she whispered to him as she pushed him down on the sofa and sat next to him.

"I can't . . ." Richard began, but was interrupted by Thomas.

"I know you'd like to, but you can't monopolize

Kitty, Richard," he said, taking Kitty by the arm. "We all want to hear her sing some of those wonderful little ditties she knows." He gave her a quick nudge towards the pianoforte.

Kitty dug in her heels. "Thomas, are you quite out of your mind? I'm sure Richard has heard me sing in times past and doesn't care to repeat the experience."

"Oh, you do have a lovely voice, Kitty." Richard was too hasty in his compliment. "It's just that after the trip today, I'm not particularly in the mood for music."

"Good, I'm certainly not in the mood for music either." With that, she glared at Thomas and started to resume her seat on the sofa. She wasn't fast enough. Thomas cut across and sat down in her place beside Richard, leaving her the opposite chair. She sat down, gave her brother a vicious look which he ignored, and was on the point of a caustic comment when Maman suggested a game of whist. Thomas bounded up, pulling Richard up with him. "Just the very thing, Maman. After sitting in a carriage all day, I'm sure Richard would welcome a friendly game."

Papa, Maman, Thomas, and Richard made up four, so Kitty elected to sit out. She wouldn't have been able to concentrate anyway, although it would have been worth her allowance to beat Thomas. Instead, she spent her time sitting next to the table trying to distract Thomas. She was only partially successful.

After what seemed an interminable time, the party broke up and they all headed upstairs. Kitty managed to get next to Richard. "I'll see you in the library in half an hour," she whispered.

"I can't do that," he mumbled back, looking around to see if anyone had heard. "It's not proper."

"Bosh," Kitty answered. "I'll be there." She went into her room and left Richard standing with a perplexed look.

At the exact half hour, Kitty opened the door to the library and peered around. She wouldn't have put it past Richard to tell Thomas, and she almost expected to find the both of them there. As it was, the library was empty. Kitty waited for almost another half hour, then crept back upstairs. She knocked softly at Richard's door. "Richard, are you there? Open the door," she whispered, knocking again as loudly as she dared.

The door opened, and Thomas was standing there, smiling down at her. "Looking for me, Kit?"

"You know very well that I wasn't."

Thomas came out and led her to her door. "You shouldn't go around knocking on strange doors in the middle of the night. It just ain't done, you know. What if Maman found out?"

"You're insufferable." Kitty wished she could use her stable vocabulary on him.

"Oh, quite," Thomas agreed, opening her door and pushing her inside. "Richard tells me you wanted him to spy for you. You didn't have to go to all that trouble. You could have asked me."

"Oh, yes. I can well imagine what kind of tale you'd spin." Her voice dripped sarcasm. "I know very well you didn't go to Portsmouth to visit the friend of a friend. You never could lie, Thomas."

"True, and that's the major flaw in my character, I believe," he said. "However, since it's you and all in the family, I'll tell you what I did today." He paused, enjoying the suspense while Kitty fidgeted. "I did go to Portsmouth, of course. I took the carriage because Richard and I picked up Captain Montfort, and the three of us went to the harbor where we got a good look at Montfort's boat."

Kitty gasped. "A boat! Of course, he'd have to have a boat for smuggling."

"Oh, Lord!" Thomas rolled his eyes upward. "There you go again jumping to conclusions. It's no surprise. Montfort had even asked Papa about docking it here until he can get a proper dock built at Sherbourne. I told you that."

"That was before I knew."

Thomas gave her a nasty look. "You don't know a thing. Montfort wanted a boat because he likes to go sailing, and he got a bargain on this one. He had it sent to Portsmouth for refurbishing." He paused. "And in case you're wondering, he plans to sail for pleasure."

"No doubt it's a boat too small for anything else." Kitty was caustic.

Thomas shrugged. "About fifty or fifty-five feet, I suppose." He turned back to the door and started to pull it closed. "I want you to get this smuggling notion out of your head. Montfort's all right and I like him."

"And that's a recommendation?" Kitty asked. "As I recall, you like opera dancers as well."

"Another thing altogether," Thomas said cheerfully. "Now to bed with you. Maybe Montfort's boat will be here tomorrow or next day, and perhaps you can persuade him to take you for a short sail."

Kitty stuck out her tongue at him as he closed the door.

The next morning, over her protestations, Bidwell dressed Kitty in a blue sprigged morning gown trimmed with a roleau of white gauze. She saw neither Richard nor Thomas at breakfast and was at loose ends. Since the day was fine, she decided to walk down to the beach while she waited on those slug-a-beds to get up. Bidwell had insisted on her blue kid slippers that matched her gown, so the walk was treacherous, and Kitty picked her way carefully over rocks and around the loose sand, keeping her eyes on her expensive slippers.

"It's a shame to have to stare at the ground on such a beautiful day." Kitty's head jerked up, and she saw Montfort standing close to her. "Would you like to walk this way, Miss Walsingham? Your father gave me permission to clear the path, so you may walk this way without ruining your slippers." He glanced at them. "Quite the height of fashion. French, are they not?"

"Yes." Kitty stared at him coldly. "Is anything wrong with that?"

"Not at all. I admire your taste," he said smoothly. "Would you like to come down to the dock with me? I'm sure Thomas told you that I had purchased a pleasure boat, and the captain from Portsmouth brought it in this morning on the tide." He smiled at her. "I'm anxious to show it off to someone."

"Yes, Thomas mentioned you had purchased a boat."

He smiled at her, a most charming, disarming smile. Kitty tried to steel herself from its attraction. It was difficult to do as the sun was making golden glints in his hair, and his amber eyes were warm and friendly. Altogether most disconcerting, Kitty thought.

"Would you like to be the first to go with me on board? Every boat needs to be christened by a visit." He smiled at her again, and Kit wished again he wasn't looking so devilishly handsome this morning. "Well, Miss Walsingham?"

Somehow Kitty found herself saying yes and found Captain Montfort escorting her down a newly cleared path to the edge of the beach. There was a trim boat moored to the dock, all newly painted and obviously renamed, her sails furled. "It's beautiful," she said, meaning it.

He was quite pleased. "Thank you. But you must come aboard and see it. I've had it redone from stem to stern, and Thomas and your father graciously said I could moor her here at your dock until I have one built at Sherbourne." He led her down the dock and across the gangplank to the deck.

"Are you a sailor, Miss Walsingham?"

Kitty was busy looking around at the immaculate scrubbed deck. "Yes. No." She turned to look at him, smiling in spite of herself. "That is, we once had a boat—that's why the dock is still here—but Papa got rid of it years ago. How I used to love to go sailing with him!" She looked out to sea, remembering. "I was just a small girl, and we would go out often. Our boat wasn't so large or so grand as this, but I thought it was the most magical thing in the world to sail on the sea."

He came to stand beside her at the rail. "I know that feeling well. I used to go sailing with my grandfather when I was a small boy." He laughed. "My grandfather had evidently wanted to be Sir Francis Drake when he was a small boy, so he passed his love of the sea on to me."

"Your grandfather was a sailor?"

He shook his head, the sun making gold streaks in his hair. "No, I'm afraid not. He always wanted to be one, but he had the responsibilities that go with the title. He had to settle for running the family estates. He was a good landlord and was very careful about his responsibility to the family and the tenants."

"Unlike some." Kitty said no more.

"Exactly. But what happened to your sailing days, Miss Walsingham? Did you outgrow them?"

Kitty looked back out to sea. "No. There was a family tragedy. I had a younger brother who was sick most of the time. Papa felt the sea air was good for him so he took Robin with us as much as possible. We got caught one day in a very sudden, terrible storm, and Papa told us to stay below. Of course, I didn't listen and crept up to see the wind and rain, and my brother followed me. There was a huge wave, and we both tried to hold on, but he wasn't strong enough. He was washed overboard." Kitty was very quiet. "Papa sold the boat shortly afterwards."

He put his hand on hers as it rested on the rail. "I'm very sorry, Miss Walsingham. I didn't mean to bring back sad memories for you."

She smiled up at him. "It was a very long time ago, and most of my memories of sailing are good ones." She glanced into his eyes and saw a strange look. Then it was gone, and his eyes were smiling and friendly again.

"But you must see my boat," he said, pulling her by the hand across the deck. "I suppose I'm inordinately proud of it, but I wanted everything done exactly right." He showed her everything from the polished brass fittings to water casks to the polished teak that made up the deck and railings. "Do you like it?" he asked after they had finished their tour.

Kitty sat down on a small bench. "Very much."

He sat down beside her. "Good. You must let me take you sailing. Perhaps one day very soon?"

"Perhaps," Kitty felt herself smiling at him. Suddenly his nearness made her seem almost breathless, and she got up and stood by the rail again. "I see you've renamed her. Why a name like *Erinys?*"

"I thought it apt. Do you know about the Erinyses?"

Kitty shook her head and he smiled at her again. "For shame, Miss Walsingham. I would have thought you to have a thorough grounding in the classics—a bluestocking almost. Your brother tells me you're quite a reader."

Visions of *Pamela* and Mrs. Radcliffe's gothics floated through Kitty's mind. "In truth, I'm somewhat weak on the classics," she said, not at all untruthfully. "Papa taught me some, of course, but my governess was more interested in watercoloring. Papa said I should read the classics on my own, but somehow I never got around to it."

"A wise man, your Papa," he said, looking down at her and smiling again. "I believe he was quite right, and I leave it to you to look up Erinyses before our next meeting."

Kitty caught her breath at the sweetness of his smile. She had to get away. "I'll be sure to do that," she said, turning to the gangplank. "Now, if you'll excuse me, I really must be getting back. Thank you for showing me the *Erinys*."

He took her arm and helped her. The touch of his hand on her arm was firm and warm. "My pleasure. Don't forget that we're to go sailing soon."

"I won't," Kitty said, glad to be off the boat and away from him. She started up the path but, to her consternation, discovered Montfort stepping beside her. "It really isn't necessary for you to walk me home," she said. "I manage quite well."

"And here I thought you were finally beginning to enjoy my company, my brilliant repartee, and, most of all, my tendency to steer clear of mud and rock," he said with a chuckle. "Be careful, Miss Walsingham. You're headed right for the wash again."

Kitty stared down at her feet. Her blue kid slippers were right on the edge of the mud. "I knew it was there," she said.

"Certainly." His voice held the slightly mocking tone she had heard when she first met him. "And, since you do not require my assistance, I take my leave." He looked down and smiled at her, his eyes turning almost dark "Don't forget to look up *Erinys*, Miss Walsingham. I plan to quiz you when we next meet."

"I won't. That is I will." Kitty felt quite confused. Why was she feeling so tonguetied? "That is, I certainly will look it up. Good day, Captain Montfort." She hurried up the path before he could say anything more. To her chagrin, she heard his chuckle behind her as she sped to the house, heedless of the sand and rocks.

Chapter Seven

Thomas and Richard were at breakfast when she returned to the house, breathless from her quick climb up the path. "A pair of slug-a-beds," she said, helping herself to a cup of chocolate.

"Only because certain people insist on roaming the halls at all ungodly hours of the night," Thomas said, while Kitty felt her face flame. Thomas looked at her and softened his words with a smile. "And where have you been at daylight?"

"It happens to be past ten o'clock," Kitty said, sitting down by Richard. "I've been down inspecting the *Erinys*."

"What's that?" Richard asked around a mouthful of muffin and strawberry jam.

"Really, Richard, you should know the *Erinys*—it's Captain Montfort's boat, of course. He gave me the grand tour."

"*Erinys*." Richard swallowed his muffin and reached for another. "I don't recall seeing that name on the boat. In fact, I don't recall seeing *any* name. What does it mean?"

Kitty smiled at him over the rim of her chocolate cup. "I'm surprised at you, Richard. You should remember enough about the classics to know all about that."

"Well, if it was connected to fallow fields or to

spreading manure, I might be able to place it. Classics don't do a farmer much good."

Thomas choked as Kitty and Richard looked at him, and then they all broke into laughter. "Richard, will we ever manage to make a gentleman out of you?" Thomas finally said.

"Never," Richard answered promptly.

They were interrupted by Maman coming into the room. "Ah, there you are, my dears. I had hoped to dragoon you into helping me today. I've decided it's a perfect day for cleaning and hoped to get you to help me supervise. I've already sent to the village for help. Kitty, dear, would you help Duff see to the silver and perhaps oversee getting the linens out?" She turned to Thomas and Richard to issue orders to them.

"You know we'd love to assist you, Maman, but we promised Papa we would ride to the village for him," said Thomas with his sweetest smile, the one that always melted Maman. He took no chances though, heading hastily out the door, pushing Richard out in front of him.

Kitty grimaced as the door shut behind them. "I hope Thomas marries a true termagant," she said. "One who tells him what to do and when to do it." She glanced down at the gown Bidwell had so carefully chosen. "I suppose there's no escape, so if I'm going to help, I'd better change clothes."

Kitty came down wearing her oldest round gown, a much frayed and sometimes patched gown of dull brown. It was quite serviceable, unbelievably hideous, and she thoroughly hated it. It was perfect for cleaning. She and Duff decided to first get out the silver and put two of the hastily recruited village girls busy polishing.

Duff cared as little for supervising the cleaning as Kitty did. After several sighs on his part and a few reminders about the state of his rheumatism and his feeble old age, Kitty let him stand and watch as she dragged the silver out and put it on a table to have the girls polish it. The silver was unbelievably dusty, and some of it had tarnished badly since last cleaning day. Before she had the girls shining the silver to her satisfaction, Kitty had spilled silver polish on her dress and her apron was dirty with tarnish.

After nuncheon, with the silver out of the way, Maman began on the rugs while Kitty turned her attention to the linens. She was busy setting in the middle of a big pile of sheets, sorting out the ones that needed to be patched and putting the others aside to be boiled and ironed.

Maman came into the room, all in a flutter. "Kitty, my dear, you seem to have company." Kitty looked up to see Maman in her gray everyday dress with a cap on her head. Right behind Maman stood Captain Montfort, his cousin Marianne, Thomas, Richard, and to Kitty's complete horror, Harriette Marlowe. Kitty glanced down at her old, frayed gown and filthy apron, then looked back at the company standing in the door. Captain Montfort had changed from the morning, and was now dressed in buff pantaloons with a pale blue waistcoat and a coat of dark blue superfine; his sister was in a fashionable green striped muslin. Kitty's gaze shifted to Harriette Marlowe, then lingered as Harriette stepped forward to see her. Miss Marlowe looked as if she had just stepped out of the latest edition of a pattern book. She was in white lawn, with an edging of fine lace and blue beaded riband around the neck. Matching ribands were threaded through her artfully arranged blonde curls. Harriette's eyes widened in surprise as she took in the details of Kitty's attire.

Kitty scrambled to her feet, dragging a sheet with

her which covered part of her dress. She adjusted her cap and pushed her hair out of her eyes with a grimy hand.

"We met the captain and the ladies out for a stroll, and Thomas thought they might want to stop by for some refreshment," Richard said, totally unaware of Kitty's mortification.

Kitty stood still and glared daggers at Thomas. Finally, Captain Montfort stepped into the breach. "My apologies, ladies. Perhaps we have come at an inopportune time . . ."

"Oh, not at all," said Thomas. "Kitty's just helping with a spot of cleaning. Doesn't signify at all. We can go on into the withdrawing room." He smiled at Kitty. "Kit, my dear, would you ring for some lemonade?"

They all trooped out, leaving Kitty still standing speechless, holding the sheet. Captain Montfort turned at the door. "I do wish you'd join us, Miss Walsingham. Perhaps you would like to come up after you, ah, tidy up?" Kitty didn't answer him and, after an awkward hesitation, he turned and followed the others.

After they had gone, Kitty threw the sheet onto the floor, then tore off her apron and tossed it down. "Blast and damme!" she said, as Duff turned and gazed at her horror-stricken. She left him with the sheets and fled upstairs.

Kitty stayed in her room and refused to answer the door when Thomas knocked. "Kit, I know you're in there. Come on and join us. You're acting like a spoiled brat." She gritted her teeth and let him stand outside. After she heard him leave, she looked in the mirror. She was a complete mess. Her cap had kept falling off, so her hair had gone every which way when she was rummaging in the sheets. Worse, she had dust and grime all over her face and arms. She looked like any cleaning girl from the village.

It was bad enough Montfort had seen her looking like this—but Harriette Marlowe! Of all the people in the world Kitty hoped never to see, Harriette Marlowe was the first. She didn't merely dislike Harriette, she loathed her. Of course, she knew she was probably the only person in all of England who didn't care for Harriette, a blonde incomparable who had been the acknowledged beauty of London for two seasons now. All Harriette had to do was lift a shapely hand, and every eligible man under eighty came flocking to do her bidding. Kitty had heard tales all last season that Harriette had to marry money, and that she was going to have to do it soon or her father was Newgate bait, but that tale had been around for a long time, and Mr. Marlowe was still gaming away every farthing he could find every night. Besides, to look at Harriette, no one could believe such a tale—she had the finest of silks and muslins for her gowns, shawls of only the best cashmere, dozens of shoes, reticules, and gloves.

Kitty sighed. Compared to Harriette, Kitty and the rest of the girls in London paled into insignificance. Nothing they could do could ever match Harriette's brilliance. And, Kit added to herself ruefully, she would wager her entire allowance that Harriette had never in her life rummaged through tarnished and dirty silver.

Kitty slipped down the back stairs and cut across the garden to the path to the beach. She simply couldn't face them, not now, not looking like this, knowing they had seen her. She went to the cliff overlooking the dock and sat down near a pile of rocks. This had been "her" spot since she was a child. She kicked off her shoes, leaned back against the rocks and looked out to sea.

"I was afraid I had lost you." The voice came from behind her. Kitty didn't answer. "Do you mind if I sit?" Montfort came and sat beside her, looking out to sea. "I was standing by the window when I saw you going across the lawns to the path leading down here." Kitty still didn't say anything. "What's wrong?" he finally asked, his voice soft.

She shook her head. "Nothing."

"Don't tell me that." He chuckled slightly. "I have four sisters, you know, and if I ever brought someone home on cleaning day without warning them first, they'd each have a turn with my head on a decorated platter. I believe I should apologize to you on behalf of all of us."

"I just . . . I just wasn't expecting . . ." Kitty stopped.

"Just not expecting company and worried about the way you look," he finished for her. "That's what my sisters would worry about." He smiled at her. "Miss Walsingham, I noticed when I first met you at the wash that you tend to look quite fetching when you're grimy." Kitty turned and stared at him. "Oh, yes. Grime quite becomes you, Miss Walsingham. And, um, bare feet as well."

Kitty felt anger and reached down and yanked her slippers on her feet. "Sarcasm isn't very becoming to you, Captain Montfort."

"Oh, I assure you that I'm perfectly sincere. That's quite a compliment, too. Grime becomes very few people." He chuckled as she bent down to remove her slippers and dump the sand out of them.

Before she could help herself, Kitty smiled back. "Good," he said. "Now will you accept my apology and promise me that you won't behead Thomas at the first opportunity?"

"I accept your apology," she said with a laugh, "but I really cannot promise about Thomas. I usually think beheading too tame for most of the things he does."

"I assure you my sisters feel the same about me. It's one of the hazards of being a brother." He smiled at her again and leaned back against one of the rocks. "This is a lovely place."

"Yes." Kitty turned her face up to the sun. "I've always loved to come here and watch the sea. Much to Grand-mère's despair, I might add."

"Ah, let me guess. She thought you would be better employed doing your watercolors."

Kitty glanced over at him and smiled. "No, my needlework. I have to admit that Grand-mère despaired about my needlework too." She looked back out to sea. "I always preferred to come out here and read if it wasn't raining."

"And if it was raining . . . ?"

She laughed. "Then I preferred coming out here and sitting in the rain. Anything was preferable to needlework." She sat up straighter and looked at Montfort. "You said you loved the sea as well. Why didn't you become a sailor?"

He laughed aloud, the corners of his eyes crinkling. "I hate to tell you, Miss Walsingham, why I chose the army over the navy. I'm sure you expect some highflown reason such as I wished to protect my country against the French or that I wished to free the downtrodden."

Kitty frowned. "Not really, a sailor could do those things. Perhaps the army was a family tradition?"

He shook his head, the sun glinting on his carelessly tousled hair. "Sorry. My family has tended to gravitate to government service or to farming. No, it was a much more mundane reason, I'm afraid."

He stopped and Kitty waited. Finally she said, "Well?"

"Are you going to make me confess, Miss Walsingham?"

"Most definitely, Captain Montfort. You've aroused my curiosity." Kitty leaned back and looked into his eyes as he smiled at her once more. Suddenly she felt almost breathless and had to look out to sea and concentrate on the water to rid herself of a strange feeling of dizziness.

"Very well, Miss Walsingham, but I want you to know that this is in strictest confidence. No one knows this except you and me." He paused for effect. "Uniforms."

"Uniforms?" Kitty was blank.

"Yes. You recall I had wanted to be a sailor for years. When I was seventeen, a most impressionable age, you must admit, my grandfather and I went to London for the king's birthday parade. I was standing on the balcony of my grandfather's town house, no doubt thinking about pirates and sailing, when a troop of dragoons came down the street. Those uniforms quite took my breath away. From that instant, I became army-mad. My grandfather bought my colors two years later." He looked at her and laughed. "So you see, Miss Walsingham, that I cannot possibly let it be known why I joined the army. Can you imagine what an *on-dit* like that would do to my reputation?"

Kitty laughed with him. "Since your reputation is at stake, you need not worry, Captain Montfort. Your secret is safe with me. I happen to think uniforms are a perfectly good reason to join the army."

"Thank you for your understanding, Miss Walsingham." He looked back out to sea, and the laughter went out of his face. "Unfortunately, Miss

Walsingham, I soon discovered that a bit of cloth doesn't make an army man. I learned to love the army and the men in my command, but the uniform didn't matter. What my uniform stood for came to matter a great deal."

"I see. You told me earlier that things were difficult in France for you," Kitty said softly.

His voice and eyes were sad as he looked at her and spoke. "No one who has not been in a war can know the horrors of it. Men I fought beside and knew as well as I knew my brother were blown to bits in front of my eyes." He stopped and Kitty fought down an urge to reach over and touch him in sympathy.

"I'm very sorry," she managed to say.

He forced himself to smile. "No, I'm sorry for bringing up such sad things to ruin your afternoon." He stood. "I must be getting back before my two ladies think I've deserted them. Would you like to go with me or do you prefer to stay? I assure you that your dress will not be noticed."

Kitty doubted that as she remembered the shock and malicious glee in Harriette's eyes. She stood to look at Montfort. "I prefer to stay here for a while. Thank you for coming out to cheer me up."

"Think nothing of it," he assured her. "When I saw how upset you were, I waited for Thomas or Richard to come out to you, and when they did not, I excused myself for a moment. As I said, I have four sisters of my own."

"It was very kind of you. Thomas would not think of such a thing."

"A typical brother." He paused. "I thought perhaps Lord Richard might come to you, though."

Kitty was surprised. "Richard! Why?"

Montfort avoided her eyes. "I hope I'm not breaking a confidence, but Miss Marlowe told me that while you were in London, you told her that you and Lord Richard had an understanding. Miss Marlowe seemed to think it only a matter of time until the two of you were ready to make an announcement."

Kitty gasped. She well remembered that time in London. Albert had been to see her that morning and had taken her for a ride in the park. There he had told her that, while he held her in the highest regard, he had decided his heart belonged to the incomparable Miss Marlowe. Kitty had been crushed and had almost stayed home from the Elliot's rout that night, but pride and Thomas had forced her to go. There Harriette Marlowe had come up to her, smiling triumphantly, and asked about Albert. Stung, Kitty had told Harriette that Albert did not signify, there had been an understanding between Kitty and Richard for years. Now, she wished there were some way to take back that remark, but there wasn't.

"Richard and I have been friends for many years," she finally managed to say to Montfort.

"My warmest congratulations. Lord Richard is a fine man," Montfort said. "Now I really must get back. Are you sure you don't wish to go back with me?"

"Yes, thank you, I'm sure." Kitty managed to smile at him. "And you should hurry, before your cousin and Miss Marlowe wonder what has happened to you. They'll be sending out search parties."

"I'm afraid Marianne is rather used to my frequent absences." He smiled at her again and turned. "Good day, Miss Walsingham," he said as he walked toward the house. Kitty stood and watched him striding along the path, his chestnut hair almost golden in the sun. The rush of emotion she felt was unexpected. Suddenly she felt like crying.

She slumped down against the rocks again and stared out to sea, not seeing the waves or the sky, her mind too much of a jumble to think.

"What have I done?" she said aloud.

Chapter Eight

Kitty slept badly that night and was late coming down for breakfast. Thomas and Richard were already there, sitting beside each other, deep in a conversation that stopped abruptly when they saw her.

Thomas scrutinized Kitty as she walked into the room. "You look wretched this morning, Kit."

"Better or worse than yesterday?" she snapped, going by him and getting some chocolate from the sideboard.

"Now don't start on me, Kit. Maman already rang a peal over me and threatened to send me to the continent for a year if I ever, in her words, dragged people in on cleaning day again. I don't know why she was so cut up about friends seeing her in her cleaning clothes."

"Fustian! How would you like for Harriette Marlowe to see you in old clothes, cleaning out the stables?" Kitty slammed her cup down on the table and sat down.

"Me? Clean the stables? Kitty, have you lost your mind?" Thomas was appalled.

Richard laughed aloud. "I'd like to see that myself, Thomas. Those brocaded waistcoats would look like something other than fashionable after that job." Richard turned to Kitty. "I thought you looked very fine yesterday, Kitty," he said gallantly. "And I must say you certainly look in high bloom this morning. Pay no attention to Thomas."

"I haven't in years," Kitty said. "And thank you for the compliments, Richard."

Thomas gave Richard an obvious nudge and a wink. Richard spoke promptly. "How would you like to go riding with me this morning, Kitty? I think the fresh air would do you good."

"What a wonderful idea," said Thomas. "Kit, do you want me to go down and tell them to saddle Beau for you?" He was already half out of his chair.

Kitty glanced from one to the other. "I'm sorry, Thomas. I believe I'll stay indoors today. All that dust yesterday gave me the megrims."

Thomas paused in mid-stride. "Don't try that tarradiddle on me, Kit. You've never had the megrims in your life."

Kitty smiled at him. "I have now."

"I do wish you'd go, Kitty," Richard said. Kitty looked at him and saw that he was looking at her the way he did when they were children, and he really wanted her to do something for him. She sighed and gave in gracefully. "Very well, Richard, if you really wish me to go, I'll be glad to. A ride may be just what I need to clear my head."

"I knew you were lying about the megrims," Thomas said.

"Thomas, how can you say such a thing?" Richard asked. "Kitty would never tell a lie." Kitty felt a guilty flush creep up her cheeks. "I don't want you to get sick, Kitty. Are you sure you feel like going riding?" Richard's voice was full of worry.

"Of course. I'd love to go riding with you, Richard. Breakfast has done me a world of good. I feel quite fine." She drained the chocolate cup. "Give me time to change."

"Hurry," Thomas said. "I'll tell the groom to saddle Beau."

"Are you going with us, Thomas?" Kitty asked.

Thomas had the grace to blush. "No, I was merely trying to be helpful." Kitty gave him an unbelieving look. "Well," he said, "even you admitted that a ride would do you good."

"Your concern is touching, Thomas," Kitty said with sarcasm, then she turned to Richard. "I'll meet you at the stables," she told him. As she went out the door, she heard Thomas and Richard congratulating each other on persuading her to ride. Something was obviously afoot.

Richard was as bruising a rider as Kitty, completely at home in the saddle. The two of them galloped at full tilt across the fields that bordered the sea. Kitty was glowing with exhilaration when they finally pulled up at the base of a cliff overlooking the Channel.

"Let's go up," Kitty said. "I want to see the finest view in all of England." She pushed her windswept hair back under the hat that matched her habit. Bidwell had insisted on the new gray. "The finest view?" Richard answered, getting down and tethering his horse. "Can't convince me of that, Kitty." He carefully helped Kitty down from Beau, and they walked together up a path to the top of the cliff, chatting companionably.

When they reached the top, the wind from the sea almost took Kitty's breath. "Look, Richard. Isn't it beautiful? Look how the sun on the water looks like little diamonds."

Richard looked over the edge. "Diamonds? If you say so, Kit. Looks more like a rough sea to me. Probably rain before long."

Kitty looked over at him. Richard was testing the

wind with his thumb. He looked exactly like an overseer planning a grain harvest. Satisfied, he turned to Kitty. "It'll rain in just a little while, I'd say. Before it does, come over here and sit down with me where we can enjoy the view."

Filled with foreboding, Kitty followed him over to a rock that someone had obviously placed in an advantageous position to see across the Channel. There was room for only two on the rock, and that was two sitting close together—very close together. Kitty sat as close to one end as possible.

Fearing Bidwell's wrath, she was careful with the folds of the gray habit as she sat, watching for sand and mud. "We should return soon, Richard," she said, noticing for the first time some clouds coming in from the west.

"Oh, we will, I assure you." His voice was hearty as he sat down next to her. There was a long silence that Richard finally broke. "Kitty, I want you to know that I have the highest regard for you . . ." he began. Kitty turned to look at him, fascinated, as he stopped and took another tack. "We've been friends for many years now, Kitty, and have always rubbed along well." He stopped again, then took a deep breath. "There's been something of an understanding between our two families, Kitty, and now . . ." He crashed his fist into his palm. "Dash it all, Kitty, you could help me with this, you know!"

"Help you, Richard?"

"Yes, help me. I don't know why I even have to go through this." His voice was irritable. "Thomas told me that you were in complete agreement. You even told everyone in London that we had something of an understanding. Miss Marlowe told me that."

Kitty's eyes narrowed. "Oh, Miss Marlowe said that?"

"Yes." Richard stood nervously and missed the sarcasm in Kitty's voice. "I must admit that I thought you were stretching things a little because I didn't know anything about an understanding, and my father didn't either."

"You asked your father?" Kitty felt faint.

He looked at her incredulously. "Of course I asked him. I thought maybe he and your father had made some arrangements when we were children. That's commonplace, you know." Kitty was too overcome to reply. When the silence stretched out, Richard continued. "At any rate, when I found out that there was no formal understanding, I must admit I was cut up about it. To tell you the truth, I thought it somewhat shabby of you to say such a thing, especially to everybody in the *ton*."

"I'm sorry, Richard." Kitty felt great relief now that everything was out in the open. She had thought he was about to offer for her. Now there was nothing for it except to tell the truth. "I truly am. I didn't think about the consequences."

"That's what Thomas told me," he said, sitting back down beside her. "And after I'd thought about it . . ."

Kitty turned to him and put her hand on his arm, interrupting him. "Richard, please don't be angry with me. We've been such good friends that I didn't even think about what such a story might do to you. I was only trying to convince Harriette Marlowe that . . ." Kitty gulped and searched for words.

"Oh, Thomas told me about *that*," he said: "Alfred, Albert? What was the name of that calfling you was on the dangle for?"

"Albert. And I was most definitely *not* on the dangle for him, as you so genteelly put it," Kitty snapped. "*And* I do not appreciate you and Thomas discussing my affairs."

He looked at her. "Well, dash it all, Kitty, you made it my business when you dragged my name into it."

"For that, I apologize." She paused and then continued, "Furthermore, if you wish, I'll make sure that everyone in the *ton* knows there is no hint of an understanding. You'll be completely free to do whatever you wish. I am truly sorry, Richard."

Richard grabbed her hand and held it. "Now, Kitty, calm down. That's not what I want at all. I started to tell you that I'd thought about this, and I realized it was a wonderful idea."

Kitty felt faint. "A wonderful idea?" Her voice faltered.

"Yes, indeed. I'm surprised I didn't think of it, by the way. So after I considered it, I told Miss Marlowe that yes, we did have an understanding, because I want there to be one, Kitty."

Kitty felt her mouth fall open, but before she could gather her wits to speak, Richard continued. "It's time I married and settled down, and I've been looking for someone just right for a while now. I wanted a good, reliable woman, one who was intelligent enough, but not too much."

"What?" The word was between a choke and a gasp.

He looked at her. "Men think about these things, Kitty. After all, no man wants to get leg-shackled for life to someone all wrong, although God knows that happens often enough." He stood and started pacing along the edge of the cliff in front of her. "As I was saying, I had been giving this some thought for a while, and hadn't been able to think of anyone who would settle for living in the country and being a good wife. I thought about . . . well, never mind."

He stopped and then paced some more. "At any rate, when I got that letter from Thomas telling me that you were willing . . ."

"*What!*" Kitty screeched and jumped to her feet, banging into Richard.

He staggered momentarily and then regained his balance. He took a long look down the edge of the cliff to the sea. "Maybe we'd better get farther back if you're going to go trying to push me off the edge," he said shakily, holding her arms and guiding her back behind the rock.

"I wasn't trying to push you, Richard," Kitty said, sitting down on the rock to face him and catching her breath. "You merely surprised me, that's all."

"Oh, you didn't know if I'd come through?" he asked, beaming. "Well, let me assure you, Kitty, when I showed Thomas's letter to my father, we both agreed that it was just the solution." Richard started pacing again, enumerating on his fingers. "First, you and I have known each other for an age; second, you come from a good family. Of course, you're mama's French, but you can't help that. Third, we've always rubbed along well." He paused and looked embarrassed. "Fourth, you're healthy and there should be, ah, no problem filling up a nursery."

Kitty stared at him openmouthed. "Nursery? Richard, let me explain. I don't think . . ."

He sat beside her and held her hand. "No need to be embarrassed, Kitty. Thomas explained everything to me, and I accept."

"You accept? Accept what?"

"Well, your proposal, of course. Now I know it ain't too regular for a brother and sister to propose to a gentleman, but all things considered, it was the practical thing to do. I would never have thought of it otherwise."

The world spun around and Kitty felt dizzy. "Richard, I'm afraid there's been some kind of misunderstanding here."

He patted her hand. "Now, don't you worry a bit about anything, Kitty. As your husband-to-be, I'll handle all the details. I plan to speak to your father this very afternoon."

Large fat drops of rain began to blow in. Richard pulled her somewhat ungallantly to her feet. "We'd better get back to Bellevoir now, Kit. Don't want to get caught in the rain and having you come down with something. Besides, I need to eat nuncheon and see about the marriage agreements. Now come along." He gave her a gentle shove down the path to where the horses were tethered, but stopped suddenly. "Look out there. Is that Montfort's boat? He'd better put to before the storm hits."

Kitty looked and could see a boat remarkably like the *Erinys* heading out into the Channel. "Maybe he's going to France," she said, half to herself. She devoutly wished she were on the boat sailing with him.

Richard shook his head and headed her down the path as the rain picked up. "Not a chance," he said. "Montfort's only a Sunday sailor. Don't believe he'd be heading for France, not even in clear weather." He hoisted Kitty unceremoniously up on Beau. "By the by, Kitty, all that smuggling nonsense you were prattling about—that's all it is, just nonsense. I assure you this part of the coast is as quiet as a church on Sunday night. Come along now."

Kitty bit her tongue down on a sharp retort at his attitude and followed as Richard led the way home. Her foul mood wasn't helped when they were caught in a deluge on the way back, and Richard turned to her saying, "Didn't I tell you it would rain?" By the time they reached Bellevoir and Kitty had dismounted in front, she was more than angry. When Duff opened the door for her, Kitty was drenched, bedraggled, and thoroughly out of sorts. Richard had gone on to the stables to take the horses, so Kitty barged in the door, passing by a scandalized Duff and leaving a trail of water behind her. "Thomas!" she screamed. "Thomas, you wretch, where are you? I want to talk to you *now!*"

Maman came out of the little yellow parlor. "Catherine, whatever are you doing? You're completely soaked!" Maman took one look at Kitty's angry face. "Is something wrong?"

Kitty stopped abruptly and made an effort to smile at her mother. "Not a thing, Maman. I merely needed to speak to Thomas for a few minutes."

Duff creaked to a halt behind Kitty. "I believe the young master has gone to Sherbourne for the day," he said.

"So that's where he's hiding," Kitty muttered.

"What, my dear?" Maman asked. "Surely whatever you need to speak to Thomas about can wait until you get out of those wet clothes. You're going to catch the ague." She looked down at the puddles slowly forming from water dripping from Kitty's habit and bedraggled hat. "Besides, dear, the floor . . ."

Kitty opened her mouth to protest, but there was no arguing with Maman. In a flash, Kitty was banished to her chamber, Bidwell was summoned to change her, and a restorative cup of chocolate had been sent up. Kitty paced the floor, rehearsing the epithets she was going to use in her conversation with Thomas when the ringing of the nuncheon bell brought another thought to her mind. She must somehow keep Richard from speaking to Papa until she could unravel this tangle. She sped down the stairs as Duff let Richard in the door.

"Richard, I must speak to you."

"Sorry, Kitty. It will have to wait. I took something of a nasty fall down at the stables."

For the first time Kitty looked at him. Richard was covered with muck from head to foot. With great relief, she smiled. "It's no laughing matter," Richard said testily. "I could have broken something."

"I'm sorry, Richard," she said, trying in vain to keep from wrinkling up her nose. Richard had evidently fallen in the worst part of the stables. "Why don't you go on up to your chamber, get the footman to pour you a nice hot bath, and I'll have nuncheon sent up to you on a tray." And that way you won't see Papa, she thought to herself.

"Wonderful idea, Kitty," Richard said, much cheered. "Be sure to send plenty to eat. A man needs a good nuncheon to hold him until suppertime." He started up the stairs. "I'm very pleased at the way you take things in stride, Kitty. Yes, I think this is going to work out quite well for both of us." He went on up the steps, whistling.

Kitty took no chances. She sent a nuncheon large enough for six up to Richard's chamber and made sure the footmen carried up enough hot water for a bath. That done, she stationed herself near the front door, waiting to pounce on Thomas when he returned. Recalling her conversation with Montfort, she decided beheading wasn't harsh enough for this particular offence. Perhaps burning at the stake.

Duff shuffled across the polished foyer and creaked to a stop beside her, regarding her from beneath bushy white brows. Kitty fidgeted as she thought of, then discarded, excuse after excuse. Duff, conditioned by years of experience, saw right through her. "Master Thomas said he would not return until late afternoon," he said, taking a position beside the door. Beaten, Kitty glared at him and went into nuncheon.

Maman was already seated, helping herself to some cold ham. "Did you have a nice ride, dear?" Maman asked. "Except for the rain, of course."

"Wonderful." Kitty's voice was morose. "Wonderful!" she corrected cheerily. Maman glanced at her sharply, so Kitty spent the rest of nuncheon carefully chattering inanely about anything and everything. She was greatly relieved when Maman announced plans to visit the vicar's ailing wife during the afternoon since the rain had stopped. Kitty waited patiently until Maman had packed a jar of her famous calvesfoot jelly and some barley water to take to the invalid.

As soon as the carriage was away from the door, Kitty ran in search of the footman who had attended Richard. A few quick questions elicited the information that Lord Richard had taken a bath, eaten heartily, and then decided to take a short nap. Kitty breathed a long sigh of relief. At last she had some time — now to head off Thomas and untangle this mess.

She announced she was going to her chamber to nap, emphasized to Duff that she was not to be disturbed, then went off up the stairs. After waiting a few moments, she slipped down the back way and picked her way across the wet grass to the path that led to Sherbourne. She stationed herself beside a big tree that had once held a swing and prepared to wait for Thomas.

All day, if necessary.

Chapter Nine

The afternoon dragged while Kitty waited for Thomas. She paced a while, sat on a rock for a while, grumbled more than a while, and waited until the shadows lengthened. Finally she gave up, breaking over and allowing herself to use a word or two she had heard from the stableboys. It gave her immense satisfaction.

Kitty banged on the knocker, and Duff opened the door with a look of surprise. "I was not aware you had gone out," he said frostily. Kitty passed him by, wishing heartily she could use one of her stable words on Duff, then headed up the stairs. Duff's rusty voice floated up the stairs behind her, "Master Thomas is in the library if you still wish to see him."

Wheeling on one foot, Kitty turned and ran down the steps. "Duff, you're a dear," she shouted over her shoulder. When she got to the library door, she squared her shoulders, rehearsed her opening line, and threw open the door. "How did you slip by me? Where have you been?" she asked angrily.

Thomas was seated at Papa's desk and he quickly, and, Kitty thought, guiltily, stuffed something back into the middle drawer. Forgetting she was come to ring a peal over him, she pounced on his hand which was still on the drawer latch. "What's that?"

she demanded. "What are you trying to hide?"

"What? Whatever are you talking about, Kit?" Thomas's voice and expression were carefully innocent, but his grip on the drawer front was ironclad as Kitty pulled on his fingers.

"What are you hiding, Thomas? I want to know."

He let go of the drawer and grabbed both of her hands, then got up, pushing her away from the desk. "Hiding? Whatever are you saying, Kitty? I'm not hiding anything."

She resisted and tried to pull away, but, to her surprise, Thomas had become amazingly strong in the past few years. "You are! I saw you trying to conceal something in the desk drawer."

Thomas sat down on the sofa and pulled her down beside him. He still held her hands. "You saw me do what?" His tone was incredulous and he stared at her guilelessly.

Kitty had seen that look a thousand times from the days when Thomas was in leading strings. "Don't you try to cozen me, Thomas. What's in that drawer?" She paused. "It has something to do with Montfort and the smuggling, doesn't it?" The thought made her sad. Since she had gotten to know him better, she had been rapidly revising her opinion of Montfort's character. Almost, just almost, she had believed Thomas that Montfort was truly innocent.

Thomas hesitated only for a second, but that was enough to confirm Kitty's suspicions. Then Thomas forced a light laugh. "Really, Kitty! There you are going all gothic on me again. Smugglers, indeed!" However, he didn't release her hands.

"Are you involved, Thomas?" she asked quietly. "It would be almost more than I could bear if you were. The very thought of it would destroy Papa and Maman."

"Kitty!" Thomas's voice was truly indignant. "What kind of lowlife do you take me for? Oh, I might take a nip on a little smuggled brandy now and then, or buy a bit of French silk or lace for a . . . for you or Maman. Everybody does that much, you know. But for you to even suggest I would be illegally involved in such a thing . . ." His voice trailed off.

"Then show me what you're hiding."

"Kitty, I'm not . . ."

Kitty interrupted him sharply. "Thomas, don't bother to deny it anymore. This is not one of your London ninnies you're speaking to. I know you better than anyone else in the world, and you never could tell a lie that I didn't see right through. Now, show me what you're hiding."

Thomas shook his head. "I can't, Kit. But I promise you that I would never be involved in anything that would harm my family or England." He stopped and looked at her. "I'll tell you about it just as soon as I can honorably do so, I promise."

Kitty searched his face for a clue, but didn't know what to think. This was a different Thomas from the dilettante who frequented the clubs and tailors of London. Older, more like Papa. "Thomas," she began, but he cut her off.

"Please, Kitty. You have my promise, but not now." He looked at her and was evidently satisfied with the expression he saw in her eyes. Then he changed the subject. "How was your morning, Kit?"

She tried to raise her hands, but he still held them. "My morning!" she sputtered. "You knew all along what Richard had in mind, didn't you?"

"Of course." He smiled broadly at her. "And may I say in all modesty that I assisted Richard in the planning and execution. May I wish you happiness?"

"No, you may not!" Kitty felt tears coming on. "I don't know!" she wailed, bursting into full-fledged sobbing. "Thomas, I am so confused."

He released her hands and patted her back, then produced a handkerchief from the depths of his waistcoat. "Kit, whatever is wrong? Did Richard manage to bungle everything? And after I told him *exactly* what to say." He mopped at her eyes. "Did the lout come a complete cropper?"

"No. Yes." Kitty took the handkerchief and scrubbed at her eyes and dripping nose.

"Well, which is it, Kit? What happened?"

She took a deep breath. "Richard offered for me."

Thomas looked at her quizzically. "Well, I knew that. And . . . ?"

"I didn't know what to say, Thomas." There was a fresh flood of tears.

He stood and stared down at her. "You didn't know what to say! Good Lord, Kit! I thought you *wanted* him to offer for you. Didn't you prate all over London about there being an understanding between the two of you."

"I didn't exactly *prate*, Thomas."

"Oh, I see! Do you mean you used Richard for an excuse and nothing else!" Thomas started pacing the library floor, walking the length of the elegant Aubusson and back. "Do you know how much talking I had to do to convince him that now was the right time for him to get leg-shackled and settle down to farming?"

"None," Kitty said through the folds of the handkerchief. "He told me he'd been thinking about it for a while."

"No matter," Thomas said hastily. He stopped in front of her. "I practically gave *my word* that you'd accept him." He stalked down the Aubusson again. "And now you've refused him. *Refused!*"

"I didn't exactly refuse, Thomas."

He stopped abruptly. "You didn't? Then by Jove, why all the fuss and tears. There isn't any problem, is there? You accepted." He smiled at her.

"I didn't exactly accept, Thomas."

Thomas's smile faded and was replaced by a scowl as he resumed his pacing. He was making an obvious effort to stay calm. "Just what did you do, Kit?"

"Nothing," she answered wearily. "Richard just seemed to assume that it was all the thing. He didn't even give me a chance to say very much."

"I suppose that was because I assured him your reply would be 'yes'," Thomas said, glaring at her.

"He's going to speak to Papa as soon as possible." She twisted the handkerchief into a sodden shred of linen. "I don't know, Thomas! I just don't know! I can hardly bear the thought of spending the rest of my life at Collingwood Hall with Richard, listening to him prose on about plows and manure. And then there's the other . . . ," she added faintly.

"Other?" Thomas sat down beside Kitty and stretched his legs out elegantly in front of him. "What other, Kit?"

She turned a furious pink. "Well, the other. I don't know if I could . . . if I wanted to . . ."

Thomas looked at her sharply and broke into laughter. "Oh, *that* other. Didn't know a country girl like you had turned missish and modest on me,

Kit."

Kit found a sudden interest in the pattern of the Aubusson until her face cooled. "What am I do, Thomas? Richard is like a brother to me. I just cannot see myself married to him."

"Of course you can, Kit. Once you get over this attack of being missish, you'll be perfectly satisfied with the arrangement. Richard's from a good family, we know him, and the two of you get along well and always have."

"Those are the same reasons Richard used."

Thomas laughed. "Of course, I gave them to him. Didn't I tell you I had been talking to him?"

Kit raised wet green eyes to his. "But, Thomas, I don't know if I love him. How can I tell?"

"Love?" Thomas raised an eyebrow, and his face assumed an expression that did more than express his distaste. "A highly overrated emotion, Kit. You've been reading too many of those novels again. Real people don't fall in love."

"Papa and Maman did," she said stubbornly.

Thomas rose and began pacing the carpet again. "They're different. Papa and Maman are . . ." He paused, thinking of a word.

"Special?" Kit supplied.

"Exactly." Thomas stopped and shook an emphatic finger at her. "Of all the couples I've seen, and believe me in London, they're legion, in every case except for Maman and Papa's, the romance has worn off within the first year, leaving two very disgruntled people who have nothing in common. Nothing, that is, except perhaps a marriage certificate and a distinct hatred of each other." He walked back and leaned against the desk. "At least you and Richard are friends at the beginning. I tell you,

Kit, that's much the best."

Kitty rose and glared at him. "Just what I needed to help me right now — pompous advice from the dilettante about town."

"Believe me, Kitty, you'll thank me for this some day. I speak only the truth."

She headed for the door, then turned and faced him. "Based on your own wide experience with love, no doubt. Thomas, the only thing you've ever been in love with is your own self. The only thing you've ever cared for is the fit of your waistcoat."

He laughed as she jerked the door open. "At least my waistcoat doesn't yell at me like a dockside fishwife," he said.

"I have every right to yell at you if I want to. If it hadn't been for you and your infernal meddling, I wouldn't be in this dilemma!"

"Don't forget your well-chosen words to Harriette Marlowe. That may have had something to do with this."

"If you were a gentleman, you wouldn't mention that!"

He smiled at her lazily. "True, Kit, but you're the one who keeps telling me I'm no gentleman."

Furious, Kitty stormed out the door. There was another laugh which she cut short by slamming the door behind her. She was all the way up the stairs before she remembered that Thomas had hidden something in the desk — something he didn't want her to see or know about. "Deliberately," she muttered. "He provoked me deliberately." She turned and went back to the library door and pushed it open. She was not at all surprised to find the library empty, the desk drawer empty, and the window facing the garden wide open. Thomas had decamped, and, although Kitty searched through every scrap of paper in the desk, she found nothing that should not be there.

Kitty looked out the window in hopes of seeing tracks, but there was nothing. She pulled the large glass window down just as she heard a noise at the door. Thinking it might be Thomas returning, she determined to catch him red-handed. She quickly dodged behind the heavy velvet drapes just as the door swung open, then fought back a sneeze as the dust from the drapes settled around her. She backed against the wall and prayed that she was sufficiently concealed. Only after there was no risk of sneezing did she dare try to peek around the drapery fringe. What she saw froze her to the spot. Her father was sitting calmly at his desk going through his correspondence, while Richard was just entering through the door.

"There you are, Sir Jerome," Richard said jovially, rubbing his hands together. "I do hope I'm not interrupting, but I do have a matter of great importance to discuss with you." Richard took a chair in front of the desk without waiting for an acknowledgement.

Kitty watched as Papa smiled faintly. She wanted to jump out from behind the drapes and stop Richard from speaking, but her body seemed completely paralyzed. Helplessly she watched.

"Do sit down, Richard," Papa said politely at the seated form as Richard crossed his legs and made himself comfortable. "Would you like some brandy?"

"Don't mind if I do," Richard said. "I might as well come straight to the point," he said as Papa poured and handed him his glass. "I've offered for Kitty, and she's said she'll have me." He stood and looked at Papa, who seemed to have choked on his brandy. "I say, Sir Jerome, are you all right?"

"Fine," gasped Papa, groping for his chair. "Would you mind repeating what you said, Richard?"

Richard tossed down his brandy, sat down again, and beamed at Papa. "I said Kitty and me have decided to get leg-shackled. It's a good arrangement, you know, and Kitty will be fine for filling the nursery at Collingwood Hall. Are you sure you're all right, Sir Jerome?" He paused as Papa choked and coughed again.

"The nursery," Papa gasped, locating his handkerchief in his pocket and mopping at his eyes.

Richard beamed. "Certainly. That Kitty's a good healthy girl." Kit herself gave a strangled gasp behind the drapes. Richard turned and stared right at the place where she was hidden, but turned back when he saw nothing. "As I was saying, Sir Jerome, we—that is Kitty and myself—are both in complete agreement on all points, so I think you and I can put a speedy end to the discussions on her dowry. Kitty and I would like to be married as soon as possible." Again Kitty gave a strangled gasp, covering her mouth with her hand to stifle the sound. She longed to jump from her hiding place and beg Papa to say something—anything—that would give her some time to sort out her feelings toward Richard.

Instead she mastered her treacherous sneezing and stood stock still. Papa had remained gravely quiet, but now he looked at Richard. "I am most mindful of the honor you do my family, but I would prefer to discuss this with Catherine and make sure she echoes your sentiments."

"Fine, fine." Richard smiled broadly and stood.

"As I said, I'm sure you'll find that Kit's in complete agreement. Yes, indeed, complete agreement. Just let me know when you want to discuss the arrangements."

Papa smiled back. "If her agreement is there, then I foresee no problem. Kitty's happiness is, of course, my prime concern."

"Mine as well, but I tell you, she'll be as happy as a lark," Richard assured him. "Why, she'll be going up to London a couple of times a year—when she's not breeding, of course—to buy gee-gaws and those fripperies women want. And then of course, she'll have plenty to do seeing to the house. Happy as a lark."

"I'm sure." Papa finished his brandy without mishap and refilled his glass. "But you do understand my position in wanting to speak to Catherine before I make any further arrangements?"

"Certainly," Richard said. "Perhaps you could talk to her right away and satisfy yourself. I, for one, would like to get a special license so we could be wed immediately."

"We'll see," Papa answered with a smile.

The room was quiet for a few moments after the door closed behind Richard, and Kitty heard the soft clink of the brandy decanter being opened and closed again. She scarcely dared to breathe.

Then she heard her father's voice. "Would you like to come from behind the drapes to discuss this, Catherine, or would you prefer to remain there while we talk?"

Chapter Ten

Kitty peered around the heavy draperies. "Is this an occasion for brandy, or would you rather have me ring for some orgeat?" he asked, looking at her gravely over the rim of his glass.

Kitty sneezed as she brushed the dust off her face. "Brandy, Papa, please." He poured her a small amount in a crystal snifter and handed it to her. Kitty took it and downed it in one gulp, then choked and coughed until tears came into her eyes. "Thank you, Papa," she gasped, sinking into the chair Richard had just vacated. It was still warm.

"I thought you might need that after the dust of the draperies."

"How did you know . . . ?"

He looked at her and chuckled. "It was the first time my draperies had given audible gasps on hearing the conversation in this room. Besides, I remembered that behind the draperies in various rooms had been a favorite hiding spot of yours years ago. Every time you got into a scrape, we could always find you hiding behind the curtains in the nursery."

"I didn't realize I was that unoriginal." She gave a rueful smile. "I assure you, Papa, that I didn't mean to eavesdrop. I was standing by the window when I heard you coming in, and I thought it was

Thomas, and . . ."

"No need to explain that, Kitty. I believe I'd rather not know. However, I do think you might have something else to explain." He looked at her, but she could not meet his eyes. "Well, Catherine?"

Kitty's only reply was a fresh flood of tears. Papa came around the desk and held her, smoothing her hair in the same way he had when she was a small child. "There, there, sweetheart, don't cry."

"I'm not!" Kitty wailed. "I never cry."

"Of course not." Papa dabbed at her eyes with his handkerchief. "There, much better. Now, could you possibly explain to your father what is going on? Have you truly accepted Richard?"

"I don't know, Papa. I didn't think so, but Richard seems to think I have."

"Do you wish to marry him?"

"I don't know." Kitty looked up at him. "Papa, I hate to sound like a pea-goose, but I truly don't know. Thomas thinks it would be an exceptional match."

"Thomas?" Sir Jerome looked puzzled. "Could you please explain how Thomas enters into this?"

Kitty ducked her head so she wouldn't have to look at him. "It's a long story, Papa."

Sir Jerome pulled another chair up beside Kitty's. "I have all afternoon if need be. Perhaps, then, I'd better hear this story from the beginning since the central character seems to be my darling daughter." He paused and looked at her, waiting. "Would you like to enlighten me?"

Kitty took a deep breath and began. She began at the beginning, her rash statement in London about the "understanding" between herself and Richard, told what she had surmised of Thomas's letter

99

and talks with Richard, and finished up with a brief account of the scene between Richard and herself during the morning ride.

"I must admit, Catherine, that very few people besides yourself could be involved in such an imbroglio," Sir Jerome said when she had finished. "Thomas seems to have made quite an impression on both you and Richard as to your sensibilities in this matter. I believe the important thing to ask yourself, Catherine," he said as he stroked his chin in thought, "is not whether Thomas approves or whether we think it an advantageous match, but whether or not you care for Richard enough to marry him."

Kitty looked at him gratefully. "Papa, I wondered the same thing, but Thomas assures me there's no such thing as love. He tells me that friendship is a much better basis for marriage than love."

Papa looked surprised. "Thomas said that?"

Kitty nodded. "He said I'd thank him for this some day."

"That remains to be seen," Papa said. Then he thought for a moment. "And just what are your feelings, Catherine? Do you believe that Thomas is right?"

"No. I want to fall in love," she said promptly, "in exactly the same way that you and Maman fell in love."

Papa smiled at her. "There you have your answer, Catherine. As for friendship, I wouldn't say at all that it's a better basis for marriage than love and affection. Perhaps there should be both love and friendship." He looked at her carefully. "Do you love Richard?"

This time she was able to meet his eyes. "I'm

truly not sure, Papa. I don't think I really love him, that is, not the way I always imagined love to be. It's true that we do rub along well together." She stopped and searched for the words. "I always thought love would be something else, something . . ."

Papa laughed. "It is, Kitty." He leaned over and kissed the top of her head. "Let's put Richard off for a few weeks until you have time to think about this, shall we?"

"Oh, yes, Papa!" Kitty couldn't keep the relief from her voice.

"I'll tell him of my decision, then. In the meantime, you give this conversation some thought. Don't do what's best for your Maman or me, or what might be best for Thomas. You must uphold the family, to be sure, but also do what is best for yourself."

"Thank you, Papa. I will." Kitty kissed him soundly on the cheek.

"Go on with you, minx," he said, with a laugh. "More often than not, there are times when I wonder what any man will do with you."

Kitty gave him another kiss and started to leave. At the door she turned and looked back. "How do you know, Papa?"

"Know what, Kitty?"

"How do you know when you're really in love?"

Papa laughed again. "You'll know, my dear, when the time comes, you'll know. Now off with you."

At supper, Richard was very formal with Kitty, and Thomas glared at her all through the removes. Kitty guessed that her father had wasted no time in informing Richard, and possibly Thomas as well, of his decision. Her guess was proven correct when Richard sought her in the drawing room after supper. "Dash it all, Kitty, what's this about having to wait?" he hissed under his breath so the others wouldn't hear. "Your father told me that he wanted you to wait a while until you married." Richard got a stubborn set to his jaw. "I told him that you were one and twenty already, and there was absolutely no need to wait."

"And Papa said . . . ?" Kitty prompted.

"He came up with some balderdash about how you had to wait until your grandmother came back before you could consider marrying. I don't see why." Richard was petulant.

"Family tradition," explained Kitty glibly, wondering just what else Papa had said.

"Well, everyone knows I'd be the last one to toss over a family tradition, but I can't see this one at all. I need to get home and see to the farm. Father and I had planned to install some new drainage ditches."

Seeing a respite ahead, Kitty consoled him. "Of course you must go back to Collingwood Hall then, Richard. I'm sure your father needs you. We all know how very important drainage ditches are to a farm."

"That they are. The tiles in the old ones are shattered beyond any repair. We need to manure the back fields as well. Dash it all, Kitty, I did want to take you back with me as my wife."

Kitty couldn't look at him. She was getting as bad as Thomas. "I'm honored, Richard, but there is the family tradition at stake. Papa is quite right."

"Damn sorry thing, if you ask me," Richard

grumbled. "At least your father did promise to write to your grandmother right away. She should be here soon, no longer than a month at most, he said."

Kitty looked horrified. "That's not very long."

"I know," he said with obvious relief. "That's the only thing that made me agree to such a harebrained tradition. Told your father that a month was my absolute maximum. That's as long as I can stay away."

"Stay away? You're leaving, then?"

"Leaving?" Richard looked at her incredulously. "No, Kit. I'm staying here until your grandmother gets here from France. We can go ahead and get the license and everything so we can be married the minute she gets here. But remember, a month's the limit."

"A month." The words faltered. Then Kitty looked up and saw Thomas bearing down on them. She quickly jumped up to arrange a table of cards before he could say anything to her. She managed to dodge Thomas for the rest of the evening, and went upstairs early, pleading fatigue and a headache, which, after the strain of the evening, was quite real.

Once in her chamber, Kitty couldn't sleep. Bidwell had laid out a nightgown and was waiting to help her into bed, but Kitty had dismissed her. She wanted to be alone for a while, just to think. The day had been full of puzzling emotions for her, and she felt she needed some time to sort them out. She lay back on her bed, fully clothed, with thoughts going through her mind, but never reaching any conclusions. After an hour or so, the candle Bidwell had placed beside her bed sputtered and died out, and Kitty lay staring into the darkness for a while, finally falling asleep.

In the middle of the night, she woke up, cold and stiff, her neck twisted at an odd angle where it had fallen over against the pillow. She got up carefully and stretched to get the stiffness out of her aching muscles, then walked over to get her nightrail. As she walked across the room with only the faint light of a small moon to guide her, she stopped suddenly. Through the open draperies of her windows that looked out over the sea, she thought she saw a glimpse of a quickly shuttered lantern. She went over to the window and watched. In just a moment, there was another flash of light, and then another. It seemed to be some kind of code using flashing lanterns. She couldn't see any answering flash, but assumed there must be one. In a trice, her stiff muscles were forgotten, and she had donned her slippers and her dark cloak. A moment later she was slipping quietly down the back stairs, dodging a creaking step to avoid waking the servants. Noiselessly she went out the back door and carefully picked her way down the newly widened path to the beach.

Close to the sea, she stopped and crouched behind a bush, taking some time to accustom her eyes to the dark. In a moment, she could make out the dark bulk of the *Erinys* floating near the dock. Close beside it were the shadows of either two or three men; she couldn't be sure which. There were bushes scattered along the path to the beach, but the beach itself was bare, so it was impossible to get next to them. But, she thought, as she looked at the bushes along the path, it was possible to get closer. Carefully, crawling on all fours, her cloak wrapped around her to hide her hair and dress, she made her way from bush to bush, keeping well hidden. Finally she was as close to the *Erinys* as she could get. By this time, she could make out the figures of three men standing beside the dock, but she was unable to see who they were.

For what seemed an eternity, she waited, crouched in the sandy soil while the men talked. Then there was a sound off to the side of her, and she froze, almost unable to breathe. A man passed by her, walking quickly. He was looking straight ahead and did not see her. Kitty held her breath as he passed by, only letting herself breathe again after he had joined the others waiting beside the boat. A knot rose in her throat as he passed—there was no mistaking those broad shoulders or that military walk. It was Montfort.

So, she had been right about him, and the knowledge was bitter now. After they had talked, she had revised her opinion of him, she had begun to see him as a man, a brother, someone who could care for others. To know that he was a common smuggler was an odious victory. She wanted to run back to her room and try to think about her certain knowledge, but there was no way to move without taking the risk of being seen and discovered. Quietly, almost not daring to breathe, she waited, looking all the while to try to discover the identities of the other three men who had signalled and waited for Montfort.

To her horror, the men began walking toward her. They stopped a few yards down the beach from her hiding place. She could hear them clearly now, although the faces were still indistinguishable in the night.

"You think that you'll be able to get it for me,

then?" Montfort asked one of the men.

"Mais, oui," the man answered with a shrug.

"Didn't I tell you we could count on him?" one of the other men said. Kitty clamped a hand over her mouth to keep from crying out as she recognized Thomas's voice. "Jacques is the best I know at his job."

"It's necessary that this be completely secret," Montfort said.

The Frenchman's tone indicated that he was offended. "I understand that," he said. "I will have to pay bribes, of course," there was another shrug of his shoulders that spoke for him, "but no one will know where the money comes from."

"Good," Montfort said. "Then you think we can expect the merchandise to be delivered soon?"

"Jacques thinks he can have it here within a fortnight," Thomas said. "I'm willing to trust him."

Montfort looked at Thomas and paused, then turned to the fourth man in the group. "And you, are you willing to go with Jacques?"

"That I am, gov'nor." This was an unfamiliar voice, but definitely a London accent. "I know my job. I watch the money and help guard the merchandise on the return trip."

"Good," Montfort said, "I think we have an arrangement, then."

"Pay me the money now," Jacques said.

Montfort shook his head. "That wasn't part of the deal we made. The merchandise first."

"I'm taking a big risk here," the Frenchman protested. "I need the money now. I need to take care of my family. After all, I might not return."

"The Frenchie's got a point there, gov'nor," the man with the London accent said.

106

"Too risky to give him all the money now," Thomas said to Montfort, as though the Frenchman wasn't standing there hearing him. "He might not deliver the merchandise."

Montfort waited only a split second. "Half now, half when you deliver," he said to the Frenchman. "That's fair enough. I'll give the money to Williams, and he'll pay you half when you get to the French coast. He'll also have plenty of money for expenses."

"And bribes," the London accent added, with a coarse laugh.

"And bribes," Montfort said. He pulled a pouch from his coat. "Here's the expense money. I'll have to go back to Sherbourne to get your payment. Wait here for me."

He and Thomas left the two others and walked up the path. Kitty tried to get closer to the ground without making a sound. "What do you think, Thomas?" Montfort asked as they came near her.

"I think it will work," Thomas answered. "Jacques seems to know what he's doing, and from what he told me, he has access."

"I hope so." Montfort sounded worried. "So many things can go wrong."

"We're at very little risk," Thomas said reassuringly. "We do stand to lose the money, or part of it anyway, but I think Williams can take care of himself, so I don't see how anyone can get hurt."

Montfort paused beside the bush where Kitty was crouching, her breath caught into a hard knot in her chest. She stiffened, waiting for him to say something to her, but instead, he turned his back to her and spoke to Thomas. "I keep telling myself that everything is going to go according to plan, but from long experience in the battlefield, I've noticed that in almost every situation something, somewhere, usually goes wrong."

Thomas laughed and clapped him on the shoulder. "Take heart, James. I have good feelings about this particular venture."

They began walking again as Montfort answered him. "Oh, I have every confidence in it working as we planned. Williams is an excellent man, and there are very few situations he can't handle. What always worries me is the variable—the something that happens that no one has counted on."

"I think we've covered every eventuality." Thomas sounded confident.

"I hope."

"Trust me, James. We'll spend evenings in years to come talking about this. In a two or three weeks, we'll be spilling champagne over the success of this venture."

"French champagne, I hope." Montfort's voice held a chuckle.

"The cost is going to be high," Thomas warned.

Montfort laughed aloud, but quietly. "The blunt I can handle. That's the least of my worries. The rewards will be worth it." The voices trailed off as the two walked out of Kitty's hearing. A quick look back at the *Erinys* showed Jacques and the Londoner, Williams, had walked down to the dock and were lounging beside the boat. Kitty waited, wondering whether to wait for Montfort to return with the money or to try to go back along the path without being seen. She was afraid that the two men by the boat might see or hear her since they kept glancing up the path, waiting for Montfort. Even worse, there was the very real fear that Montfort would intercept her as she made her way up the path. She elected to wait.

The wait was agonizing and seemed to last forever. Her muscles cramped in the damp sea air, and a chill went right through her cloak which had been made for fashion, not for crawling around the beach in the dead of night. She had to remain still and unmoving when all she wanted to do was get up and scream and rant. The thought of Montfort being involved was bad enough, especially now that he had shown Kitty there was a good side, a kinder, more understanding side to him.

How could she have been so taken in by him? Now the worst had happened—he had dragged Thomas in with him. There was no possibility now that Kitty could go to the magistrate with her story. It would destroy Papa and Maman if everyone—if *anyone*— knew that Thomas was involved. For the second time that day, Kitty felt completely confused.

She was almost frozen from the cold, and her legs were cramping horribly when she heard the crunch of sand behind her. Quick footfalls passed by her, and in a moment the two men joined Montfort on the beach. Kitty saw a purse passed from Montfort to Williams and then in a moment, the two men had faded into the mist along the edge of the sea. Montfort walked down to the side of the *Erinys* and stood there, looking out across the Channel in the direction of France. For a wild moment, Kitty considered running down to the beach and confronting him as he stood there, but she fought down the impulse. She had to think of Thomas.

As the moon came out from behind a cloud, she saw Montfort leave the side of the ship and go the long way towards Sherbourne, a path worn along the edge of the beach. As soon as he was out of sight, she allowed herself a long sigh, and then stretched full length along the ground. Her legs and back cramped and protested with pain. Kitty bit her lip to keep from crying aloud.

After a few minutes the circulation had returned to her muscles and she sat up. Slowly she went up the path; the way clearer now with the light from the moon showing the way. At the top, at the rocks where Montfort had come and talked to her, she stopped and sat down again. She pulled her knees up to her chin and sat, looking out at the moon shining on the water that led to France. "Oh, Thomas," she murmured. "How could this have happened?" Thomas had evidently been taken in by Montfort. Kitty could understand it. She herself had been almost fooled by his veneer of charm, his expressions of concern. She had almost decided that she had misjudged him. He had seemed for a few moments to be a man of great caring, a man she might confide in, a man who would understand her.

It was bitter to realize that it had all been a sham. Probably he had been allaying her fears so that he could entice Thomas and continue with his plan without interference. He had to be stopped, that much was clear. What was unclear was just how she was to stop him. At least he didn't suspect that she knew anything.

Kitty sat for a while looking at the sea, not really thinking, just feeling. She had, she admitted to herself, been attracted to Montfort for a little while. She tried to analyze it, but got nowhere. Perhaps, she thought, the attraction was there only because she knew that Montfort was probably going to marry Harriette Marlowe. Perhaps, she thought bitterly, Thomas was entirely right when he said that it was better to be with someone who was a friend. Richard would never entice Thomas into anything as low as smuggling.

But the fact was that Thomas was involved, and heavily involved if his conversation with Montfort was any indication. What Kitty had to do was find a way out for him. After a while, she gave up thinking about it since there seemed to be no answer. Wearily she got up and walked slowly back to the house. There was a heavy morning mist coming, and the moon slowly faded behind the cloud, like a lamp behind a curtain.

As she reached the back entrance, Kitty reached up and felt her face. She wasn't sure if the water on her fingers was from the mist or from tears.

Chapter Eleven

By the time Kitty fell into an exhausted sleep, the mist outside her window had whitened into early morning. She awoke late in the morning with a splitting headache. Bidwell applied cloths and gave her drops, but she was still quite unwell when she went downstairs for nuncheon.

"Under the weather?" asked Thomas cheerily as she went to the table.

Kitty glanced at him. He showed no effects at all of his night at the beach. If anything, he looked better than usual. "I have a headache," she explained, staring with distaste at the food spread out before her.

"Ah, there you are, Richard," Thomas said as Richard made his appearance, followed by Maman and Papa. "I wondered where you had gotten off to this morning."

"Your parents and I have been talking," Richard said, with a significant glance at Kitty. He sat down next to her. "Are you ill, my dear?"

Kitty felt herself blush. "Just a headache," she mumbled.

"Good, good," Richard said heartily, patting her hand. "That is, I'm glad it's nothing worse. Don't want you getting sick now, do we?"

"Of course we don't." It was Thomas, smirking at

The Publishers of Zebra Books Make This Special Offer to Zebra Romance Readers…

AFTER YOU HAVE READ THIS BOOK WE'D LIKE TO SEND YOU
4 MORE FOR *FREE* AN $18.00 VALUE

No Obligation!

ONLY ZEBRA HISTORICAL ROMANCES "BURN WITH THE FIRE OF HISTORY" (SEE INSIDE FOR MONEY SAVING DETAILS.)

MORE PASSION AND ADVENTURE AWAIT... YOUR TRIP TO A BIG ADVENTUROUS WORLD BEGINS WHEN YOU ACCEPT YOUR FIRST 4 NOVELS ABSOLUTELY *FREE* (AN $18.00 VALUE)

Accept your Free gift and start to experience more of the passion and adventure you like in a historical romance novel. Each Zebra novel is filled with proud men, spirited women and tempetuous love that you'll remember long after you turn the last page

Zebra Historical Romances are the finest novels of their kind. They are written by authors who really know how to weave tales of romance and adventure in the historical settings you love. You'll feel like you've actually gone back in time with the thrilling stories that each Zebra novel offers.

GET YOUR FREE GIFT WITH THE START OF YOUR HOME SUBSCRIPTION

Our readers tell us that these books sell out very fast in book stores and often they miss the newest titles. So Zebra has made arrangements for you to receive the four newest novels published each month.

You'll be guaranteed that you'll never miss a title, and home delivery is so convenient. And to show you just how easy it is to get Zebra Historical Romances, we'll send you your first 4 books absolutely FREE! Our gift to you just for trying our home subscription service.

BIG SAVINGS AND FREE HOME DELIVERY

Each month, you'll receive the four newest titles as soon as they are published. You'll probably receive them even before the bookstores do. What's more, you may preview these exciting novels free for 10 days. If you like them as much as we think you will, just pay the low preferred subscriber's price of just $3.75 each. *You'll save $3.00 each month off the publisher's price.* AND, your savings are even greater because there are never any shipping, handling or other hidden charges—FREE Home Delivery. Of course you can return any shipment within 10 days for full credit, no questions asked. There is no minimum number of books you must buy.

4 FREE BOOKS

TO GET YOUR 4 FREE BOOKS WORTH $18.00 — MAIL IN THE FREE BOOK CERTIFICATE TODAY

Fill in the Free Book Certificate below, and we'll send your FREE BOOKS to you as soon as we receive it.

If the certificate is missing below, write to: Zebra Home Subscription Service, Inc., P.O. Box 5214, 120 Brighton Road, Clifton, New Jersey 07015-5214.

FREE BOOK CERTIFICATE

4 FREE BOOKS

ZEBRA HOME SUBSCRIPTION SERVICE, INC.

YES! Please start my subscription to Zebra Historical Romances and send me my first 4 books absolutely FREE. I understand that each month I may preview four new Zebra Historical Romances free for 10 days. If I'm not satisfied with them, I may return the four books within 10 days and owe nothing. Otherwise, I will pay the low preferred subscriber's price of just $3.75 each; a total of $15.00, *a savings off the publisher's price of $3.00.* I may return any shipment and I may cancel this subscription at any time. There is no obligation to buy any shipment and there are no shipping, handling or other hidden charges. Regardless of what I decide, the four free books are mine to keep.

NAME _____

ADDRESS _____ APT _____

CITY _____ STATE _____ ZIP _____

TELEPHONE (___) _____

SIGNATURE _____ (if under 18, parent or guardian must sign)

Terms, offer and prices subject to change without notice. Subscription subject to acceptance by Zebra Books. Zebra Books reserves the right to reject any order or cancel any subscription. 109002

GET FOUR FREE BOOKS
(AN $18.00 VALUE)

ZEBRA HOME SUBSCRIPTION
SERVICE, INC.
P.O. BOX 5214
120 BRIGHTON ROAD
CLIFTON, NEW JERSEY 07015-5214

AFFIX
STAMP
HERE

her. He always knew just what she was thinking. Kitty glared at him. "After all, Kit, you're going to need a good bit of stamina to do all those wedding preparations. Trousseau, linens, what have you."

"Please, Thomas." It was Maman. "Obviously Catherine does not feel like discussing this today."

"I certainly don't." Kitty gave Maman a grateful look.

"Well, I for one am sorry you're sick, Kit," Thomas said. His voice was falsely cheerful. "Montfort asked all of us over for the afternoon, and now you won't feel like going. He wants us to see some new horseflesh he has at his stables."

"And how could that possibly interest you?" Kitty asked rudely. "Are his horses done up as tulips of fashion?"

"Catherine, please." It was Maman again. Thomas smiled at her sunnily. That smile always worked with Maman.

"By Jove, I'd like to see that!" It was Richard, speaking around a mouthful of fricassee. "Montfort said the other day that he was thinking of having his man in London buy him some prime goers. The captain already has the best horseflesh in the country, to my way of thinking."

"Certainly," Thomas agreed, as if he knew what he was talking about.

Richard followed the fricassee with some bread and a glass of wine. "When are we going?" he asked.

"I thought this afternoon, that is, we'll all go if Kitty is well enough to go with us. Otherwise, it'll be just the two of us."

Richard took another piece of bread and looked at Kitty as his wine glass was being refilled. "She don't need to go, do you, Kit? You don't need to worry your head about horses." Richard turned back to

Thomas. "There, it's all settled. You and I can go on over this afternoon."

Thomas looked at Kitty. "I'm glad you agreed, Kit," he said smoothly. There was an undercurrent of laughter in his voice. "I'd hate to miss a guided tour of Montfort's stables."

"You'll fit right in," Kitty snapped.

"Catherine!" Maman was scandalized.

Thomas smiled at Maman again. "Pay her no mind, Maman. Kitty's just jealous. I suppose I'll have to offer to coordinate her trousseau for her. Pick out all the right colors and so on."

"Good idea," Richard offered, speaking quickly as he spooned up blancmange. "Might get things done quicker that way."

Kitty glared at all of them, wishing she could tell Thomas what she knew and why she was out of sorts. Papa sensed her mood. "Would you like to go up and let Bidwell put you to bed, Kitty?" he asked softly. "We'll have nuncheon sent up to you, and I'm sure that Thomas can arrange an outing to Captain Montfort's stables for you some other time."

"Yes, thank you, Papa," she said, dangerously close to tears. She got up and fled upstairs to her chamber where Bidwell fussed over her. "I told you that you shouldn't go down until you felt better," Bidwell said, dosing Kitty with some laudanum drops. "You've got to save your strength for your wedding."

"And how did you find out about that?" Kitty asked, knowing full well the servants always knew everything, usually even before the family knew. They not only knew, but, when belowstairs, discussed whatever it was completely.

Bidwell looked at her and put another cloth to her forehead. "I have my ways," she said.

The laudanum drops began taking effect before

Kitty could reply. With a muffled sigh, she fell into a deep sleep, not waking until late in the afternoon. Bidwell checked her forehead, sent downstairs for some broth and some cold meats, then forced Kitty to eat. Much as she disliked admitting Bidwell was right, Kitty did feel immeasurably better after she had supped. The problems were still there, but at least the headache was gone. Now she could spend some time wondering what to do.

Over Bidwell's protests, Kitty decided to go down for supper. Bidwell did manage to make her look more than presentable in a pale green sarsnet with a darker green braid and matching ribands in her hair. A little rouge artfully applied and Kitty looked almost her usual self.

She came into the drawing room as everyone gathered to go into the dining room. "Well, what's this? The invalid returns." Thomas peered at her through his quizzing glass, his eye looking distended. "Looking quite in the pink again, Kitty. I take it your headache has gone."

"The pain has gone, but you're still here, Thomas."

He grinned at her and offered her his arm. "I asked for that one, didn't I?"

"See here, Thomas. I ought to be the one to escort Kitty in to dinner," Richard said, looking somewhat pained. "After all . . ."

"By all means, Richard," Thomas answered, relinquishing her arm. "However, I predict there will come a day when you'll be more than glad to give that sharp-tongued chit back to us."

"Really, Thomas," Maman said. "Mind your manners."

The banter continued throughout the meal. Kitty found herself beginning to forget the night before and Thomas's involvement with Montfort. Thomas was outdoing himself to entertain them, being witty, urbane, and altogether charming. Only Kitty knew that it was an act.

Talk turned to the outing at Montfort's stables. "A prime pair of horses," Richard said. "I complimented Miss Montfort on her cousin's taste."

"Miss Montfort seemed quite good company," Thomas noted.

"Yes, indeed," Richard said with enthusiasm. "She's extremely sensible and knows more than anyone would expect a woman to know about farming. She's stayed in the country most of her life, she told me."

Thomas raised a quizzical eyebrow. "Too bad she's somewhat plain. Looks a great deal like old Sobey."

"As usual, you place too much emphasis on looks, Thomas. I thought Miss Montfort seemed quite charming," Kitty said. "Richard is quite right."

Richard preened at this confirmation of his opinion, while Thomas laughed aloud. "Practicing on echoing Richard's sentiments already, Kit?" He saw she was getting ready to ring a peal over him and continued without letting her say anything. "Well, you'll have a chance to enjoy the charming Miss Montfort's company at great length. Richard and I accepted an invitation for all of us to go sailing on Montfort's boat tomorrow."

Kitty couldn't believe her ears. Thomas was so casual about discussing Montfort and his boat. Besides, there was the small matter of Harriette Marlowe. "Really, Thomas, you should have consulted me before accepting. I can't go."

"Nonsense, Kitty. The outing will do you good. You've been staying in overmuch lately." Papa was firm. "You've always enjoyed sailing, and I think you should go."

"Yes, Papa," Kitty muttered through clenched teeth

while Thomas smiled broadly at her.

"Be sure to wear something fetching," Thomas added. "Miss Marlowe was particularly enthusiastic about going as she had a new dress to wear for such an occasion."

The next morning Kitty rose early. She had stayed up until past midnight to see if there was any activity on the beach, but there had been nothing. She hadn't been particularly surprised since Jacques and Williams hadn't had time to do very much. She judged that it would probably be at least three or four days before there was any possibility of anything happening. Perhaps even longer, depending on the type of goods they were smuggling. After all, Thomas himself had told Montfort it would be two or three weeks before they were drinking champagne.

She had reluctantly told Bidwell about the sailing trip, and Bidwell had been overjoyed, staying up late in order to ply her needle in a complete refashioning of Kitty's blue and white dress. Bidwell had pronounced it just the thing. To be sure, she had done an excellent job with it, applying blue braid to the white and giving it something of a military air. With a bonnet to keep off the sun, and a shawl for any breezes, Kitty would be at least presentable, though she had no hopes of outshining Harriette Marlowe.

She had always been an excellent sailor, so she had no qualms about eating a hearty breakfast before they left. Thomas, she noted with satisfaction, contented himself with some dry toast and coffee. Thomas sailed only slightly better than he rode.

They were to meet Captain Montfort and his party at the *Erinys*. They got there somewhat early, and Thomas led them onto the boat as if he were quite familiar with it. He spoke to the crew and they returned his greeting. Kitty noted that there was an easy familiarity there. "Thomas," she said in a low voice meant for him alone as they leaned over the railing, looking out to France. "I believe we need to talk about some things."

"Don't bother. Papa already rung a peal over me. Said that what was between you and Richard was none of my business. I told him I was only trying to be helpful." Thomas looked at her and grinned. "He said being helpful seems to be a hallmark of our family, but most people just called it being a busybody."

Kitty grimaced slightly. It occurred to her that perhaps Thomas was saying more to her than his words indicated. She looked at him, but he was still smiling at her. "Thomas," she began again, but suddenly his gaze shifted. "Here they are," he said cheerfully, leaving his post at the railing to wave at the others. Kitty thought him a little too prompt to assist Harriette Marlowe onto the deck, but perhaps she was being overly missish. She noted with approval that Richard assisted Miss Montfort.

Harriette Marlowe swept down upon her. "Dear Miss Walsingham, Thomas told us that you were indisposed yesterday. I'm delighted you're well enough to join us today." Her smile was on her lips, but never reached her eyes. Those lingered on Kitty's face, then swept up and down, taking in every detail of her blue and white dress, her bonnet, and her shawl. Evidently satisfied that Kitty's dress in no way outdid her own, she continued. "I told Captain Montfort that I would rather stay at Sherbourne than go on an outing knowing you were indisposed at home."

"Thank you," Kitty murmured. There was really nothing she wished to say to Harriette unless she could inform her that, however elegant Miss Marlowe might be for a promenade in London, she was quite overdressed to go sailing. Harriette was in a dress of canary and black striped *gros de Naples*, with flounces on the hem. She had on a hat of canary straw decorated with several large canary and black feathers, and carried a dainty yellow parasol which was trimmed with black fringe. Kitty rather hoped a sea bird would swoop down to investigate those canary and black feathers.

"We're glad you could join us, Miss Walsingham." It was Miss Montfort. "Our sailing wouldn't have been the same without you."

"Thank you," Kitty said again, only this time with warmth. "I'm delighted to be able to go with you. I had hoped we would get better acquainted." She genuinely liked the plain Miss Montfort.

"Oh." It was a strangled cry from Harriette as the boat gave a lurch. "Don't worry, Miss Marlowe," Kitty said, trying to keep the satisfaction out of her voice. "The crew is merely casting off."

In a very few minutes, they were under way, the boat cutting smoothly through the waters of the channel. In a very few minutes as well, Harriette was searching in her reticule for her vinaigrette, and looking more than a little green. Thomas, a sailor of much the same stripe as Harriette, escorted her to a bench where they both sat, looking thoroughly miserable.

Montfort wished to return to shore, but both Harriette and Thomas overrode his protests, insisting they were quite in fine feather. Neither of them sounded convincing, but with their encouragement, Montfort decided to continue the outing.

"I am so glad your brother is looking after Miss Marlowe," Miss Montfort said, standing beside Kitty on the deck. "It's very good of him to sit with her."

Kitty laughed aloud. "I'm afraid you attribute high motives to Thomas that aren't there. He's sitting with Miss Marlowe because he doesn't dare to get up. Thomas is no sailor."

"Oh." There was a pause. Then Miss Montfort caught herself. "Still, it is a nice gesture. I had no idea that Miss Marlowe had never sailed," she explained. "She's told James several times that she adored sailing."

Kitty lifted an eyebrow. "Perhaps Miss Marlowe finds it possible to adore sailing without having done it." She looked at Miss Montfort's shocked face. "I'm sorry, Miss Montfort. I didn't mean to speak harshly of your friend."

"We are rather new acquaintances," Miss Montfort said. "James introduced us, but I understand you and Miss Marlowe were already quite good friends."

"Hardly," Kitty said dryly. "Miss Marlowe and I couldn't be termed good friends. We know each other slightly." Kitty lifted her face to the breeze. "Isn't the sea wonderful, Miss Montfort? Smell the salt air."

"Call me Marianne, please, and I would be honored if I could call you Catherine."

Kitty laughed. "Only my father and mother ever call me Catherine. I much prefer Kitty." She turned back to the sea. "I love this smell and this feeling. Skimming over the waves like this is almost the way I think a bird must feel when it's flying."

Montfort spoke behind her. "Spoken like a true sailor, Miss Walsingham. But then, you did tell me before that you were once a good sailor." He came up to the rail to stand beside her as Marianne moved away to talk to Richard.

Kitty paused before she dared to answer, trying to sort out her conflicting emotions. She really didn't feel comfortable with him standing so close to her. He spoke again. "Are you missing France? I've noticed that you keep looking toward the French shore."

"No, Captain Montfort," she said crisply. "The French shore just happens to be on this side of the boat. If we were going the other way, I'd be looking at England." She took a deep breath. With Montfort this close, she was having trouble breathing. "As for me missing France, it's difficult to miss a place that I know only as a visitor. I assure you that I am most thoroughly English."

He leaned on the rail so he could see her face, propping himself on his elbows. "I thought as much," he said with a grin. "You're much too straightforward to ever be French. No offense to your esteemed ancestors, but I find the French much too devious for my taste."

"I thought your taste was French," Kitty answered without thinking.

"Ah, I understand you." He looked genuinely amused. "Thomas told me that you think me quite a scoundrel. Involved, how shall I say, in clandestine activities."

Kitty felt her face flame. Drat her brother and his mouth anyway! She bit her lip as she thought about how to answer him. "In for a penny, in for a pound," she thought to herself. She looked at him to accuse him, but found herself looking right into his dark amber eyes. The sun was shining on his hair, putting golden glints in it that matched the glints in his eyes. Kitty took a deep breath to compose herself. "I regret that Thomas mentioned something that he should have kept to himself . . . ," she began.

"Oh, we found it quite amusing."

"Really?" Rage welled up in Kitty, and she found herself forgetting her good intentions to be calm and rational. "Since you brought up the subject of clandestine activity, as you put it, Captain Montfort, I shall just ask: are you involved?" She looked directly at him, right into the depths of those amber eyes. To her satisfaction, a touch of red stained his cheekbones, and he averted his eyes.

"That depends on your definition of clandestine activity, and on whom you ask," he said, regaining his composure and assuming the mocking tone she had heard before. "I admit some have thought me quite a scoundrel," he said with a smile. "And in some cases, they may have been right."

Kitty looked at him again, hoping to see the truth in his face or in his eyes. "I had thought so at the beginning, but then I almost revised my opinion. However, circumstances have forced me to return to my original conviction."

"Are you calling me a scoundrel, Miss Walsingham?" His voice was cool and mocking. "And would you mind telling me just what circumstances prompted you to return to your original opinion?"

Kitty started to answer when she was interrupted by Marianne and Richard coming up to them. "Oh, James," Marianne said, taking Kitty's arm. "Lord Richard has just told me that we are to wish him and Miss Walsingham—Kitty—happy. They are to be married as soon as possible!"

"Really?" Montfort's expression was unreadable, but his voice was the same—cool and mocking.

To Kitty's surprise, Richard began to protest before she could. "Not exactly as soon as possible, Miss Montfort," he said, looking somewhat embarrassed.

"True," Kitty agreed quickly. "We plan to wait for several weeks at least, a month, perhaps even months."

"Quite right," Richard said, running his finger

around his neckcloth and quite effectively ruining it. It seemed to be suddenly too tight. "There's no rush at all. None."

"Oh, you must have hundreds of things to do," Marianne said.

Richard reddened. "Hundreds," he mumbled.

"Isn't that wonderful, James?" Marianne asked. "I do love weddings," she confided, turning to Kitty without waiting for an answer from Montfort.

"Weddings? There is to be a wedding?" It was Harriette, making an exceptional recovery from her bout of *mal de mer*. She dragged Thomas along with her as she joined the group at the railing. "Who's speaking of weddings?"

Richard and Kitty stared at each other miserably. Marianne smiled at both of them and answered. "Miss Walsingham and Lord Richard are getting married shortly. Isn't that wonderful?"

Harriette frowned. "Then the two of you really did have an understanding?"

"Of course," said Kitty at the same time that Richard said, "Not really." Richard was looking worse for the wear.

Thomas covered the contretemps. "Kitty and Richard had an understanding many years ago. Sort of a family understanding." He took Harriette's arm. "I'm sure you understand all about these things, Miss Marlowe."

Harriette gave Montfort a sidelong glance. "Oh, certainly. And weddings are such wonderful events." She turned to Kitty. "Have you planned some time in London shopping for your trousseau? If you have, perhaps we could go together. Wouldn't you love to assist Miss Walsingham, Marianne?"

Before Marianne could nod agreement, Harriette had turned back to Montfort. "Dear Captain Montfort, I'm sure you must allow Marianne to stay with you in London for some weeks so we can do the shops and meet Miss Walsingham." She batted her eyelashes at him in a way Kitty found particularly revolting. "Please say yes, Captain Montfort." She pouted a little in a childish fashion.

"I would never dare to deny both you and Marianne, Miss Marlowe," Montfort said gallantly, giving a slight bow. "Of course Marianne must stay in London. Perhaps when Miss Walsingham is there, we can arrange some entertainment as well as your shopping."

"And I'll be glad to help arrange the entertainments," Harriette said, then remembering herself added, "if you don't think it too forward of me."

"Of course not." Montfort seemed distant. He gave Kitty a close look, then excused himself to confer with the captain and crew.

Richard, Marianne, Harriette and Thomas wandered back to the bench on the deck to discuss plans for going to London. Kitty was left again alone beside the rail. How much had happened in just a few moments, she thought. Montfort had discovered what she thought of him, and had almost, *almost,* told her something of importance. Of that she was sure. If only Marianne and Richard hadn't interrupted him!

As she gazed out to sea, one other thought bothered her. Why was she so disturbed when Montfort had discovered that she and Richard would probably be married? Kitty tried to sort out her feelings, but they were in a jumble. All she knew was that, however much she might think Montfort a scoundrel and a smuggler, she still wished him to think well of her. It was a contradiction she didn't wish to pursue.

Chapter Twelve

Kitty sat alone that night in her room after supper. Thomas and Richard had once again gone to Sherbourne. Kitty had been invited, but had begged off, pleading a sudden headache. Both Thomas and Richard had looked at her in surprise—Kitty was never ill, and this was twice she had used this excuse. In truth, she didn't have a headache, but she had no desire at all to visit either of the Montforts or Harriette. Neither did she want to ask herself whom it was she didn't wish to see—Montfort or Harriette.

Maman had mentioned Richard's offer as the three of them—Papa, Maman, and Kitty—sat alone eating supper, adding her opinion that she felt Richard should be with Kitty instead of off gadding about the country. Evidently, as far as Maman was concerned, Richard's stock as an attentive suitor was in the decline. A warning look from Papa turned the conversation back to trivialities, but Maman seemed to have Richard and Captain Montfort on her mind. "Did you have a good day sailing?" she asked. "And just how is Captain Montfort's boat?"

"Fine," mumbled Kitty.

Maman was not deterred. "What kind of strange name was it? The *Erin*? Is he of Irish extraction, perhaps?"

Papa laughed aloud. "Marie-Louise, you are priceless! No, my dear, he is not of Irish extraction, and the name is not the *Erin*. It is the *Erinys*, the name of one of the Greek furies."

"Oh," Maman said, delighted to have comprehended, "he's named his boat for a storm."

Papa shook his head. "No, my dear. The furies were the Greek goddesses of revenge. Captain Montfort probably has intended some symbolism in naming his boat."

"How very ridiculous," Maman said. Kitty had to agree.

Dropping Captain Montfort as an uninteresting subject, Maman quizzed Kitty. "Thomas seems to have been avoiding the village lately. I saw Mrs. Braithewaite there, and she made a point to ask us all to visit. I could scarcely believe it, but I do think she has Thomas in mind for her daughter."

Kitty rolled her eyes to the ceiling. "Poor Barbara. Maman, she's been dangling after Thomas for years."

"Catherine, are you sure of that?" Maman's astonishment was genuine. "That would not be at all suitable, you know."

"I know, Maman. So does Thomas. That's why he's been avoiding the village. I think Barbara's mother watches the roads in and accosts him every time he goes there."

"That poor child."

"Thomas? A poor child?"

Maman shook her head. "Non, I meant Barbara. She must have a terrible life with parents like those. Do you know they intend to take her to London for a season? Mrs. Braithewaite told me so."

"Good Lord," Papa said. "They must be out of their minds. No matter how much money

126

Braithwaite throws around, the *ton* will never accept Barbara. He'd be better off trying to marry her to a merchant."

"Quite right, dear," Maman said. Then dismissing the Braithwaites, she turned her attention to Kitty again. "Do you think Thomas may be interested in Miss Montfort?"

The suggestion was so unexpected that Kitty choked on her food. "Miss Montfort!" she finally sputtered. "Why ever do you think so?"

"In case you haven't noticed," Maman said archly, "Thomas is spending a great deal of his time at Sherbourne. He couldn't be going over there to see Miss Marlowe as I hear that Miss Marlowe and Captain Montfort are ready to make an announcement." Kitty gave a gasp as her breath caught in her throat. Richard had suggested as much, but it was surprising to hear that it was public knowledge. Maman gave her a strange look and continued. "Since Miss Marlowe is spoken for, that leaves only Miss Montfort unattached." Maman frowned slightly. "However, I'm not at all sure that Thomas is ready for an attachment."

Kitty smothered a laugh while Papa coughed quietly into his napkin. When they finally regained their composure, Kitty agreed with Maman. "I'm glad you think so," Maman said, "because I have felt that Thomas needs more responsibility." She turned the full force of her blue eyes on her husband. "Jerome, you really need to talk to him about securing some sort of post. Perhaps Thomas would excel in government."

Papa choked in earnest, and Kitty and Maman were forced to ply him with several glasses of water and wine. "Good God, Marie-Louise," he finally managed to say. "Do you realize what you're suggesting? Thomas in charge of *anything* in the government?"

"Thomas is perfectly capable," Maman answered indignantly. "He merely hasn't had an opportunity to show anyone all the things he's capable of."

"Oh yes, he has," Kitty said.

Maman gave her a severe look. "Thomas just needs some responsibility." She looked at Papa. "I think you should talk to Captain Montfort about a position for Thomas. Miss Marlowe told me that the captain had very good connections with the government."

Kitty raised a questioning eyebrow. "Maman, perhaps Miss Marlowe was not in possession of all the facts about Captain Montfort," she suggested gently.

"Of course she was. After all, she hinted that she and the captain are to be married very soon, so surely she would know all about him, especially about his connections."

"My dear," Papa said, "when you agreed to marry me, did you know all about me?"

Maman thought a moment, then smiled. "I knew everything I needed to know, my dear."

"I don't think Miss Marlowe is in exactly the same situation," Kitty said, with more than a touch of acidity.

"Perhaps not," Maman said, signalling for the final remove, "but I still think it a very good idea for Thomas to be acquainted with Captain Montfort. I do hope, though, that he doesn't form an attachment for Miss Montfort. It wouldn't be at all the thing, especially with Thomas just starting out in government. Perhaps later."

Kitty and Papa exchanged a resigned look and turned the conversation to other topics.

Richard and Thomas returned early from Sherbourne and made a great show of going to bed early. As a result, the entire household was bedded down well before midnight. Kitty lay in bed thinking. She tried to analyze Captain Montfort but got nowhere. Was he a gentleman as Thomas insisted; was he the caring, understanding man she had glimpsed, or was he a complete charlatan who had duped her brother, or worse, was he perhaps even a criminal? He seemed to have more than his share of facets to his character. He also seemed to have completely taken in Maman, and from past experience, Kitty knew that very few people ever fooled Maman, who, despite her tendency to go off every which way in conversation, was quite a good judge of character.

Yet, Kitty had the evidence of her own eyes and ears to tell her that Montfort was engaged in something illegal, and had dragged Thomas down with him. Even if she left aside the question of Montfort's character, there was a problem that had to be solved immediately: how could she stop the whole operation without getting Thomas's name involved? She wrestled with the question a dozen ways, turning it this way and that, but at the end of a long, agonized period of tossing and turning, she still didn't see a solution.

The chiming of the clock in the hall told her it was one o'clock, and she lay back and tried to concentrate on going to sleep. She stiffened as she heard a creak, and then another. She lay very still, every sense tuned to the sounds. She heard the soft creaking again, accompanied by a whispered "Ssshhh." This time she recognized the sound as the creak of the hinges made by the chamber door to Thomas's room. It had creaked that way for years, since he had slipped out to smoke and meet the village girls after dark. That had been years ago, and Kitty still smiled to herself when she remembered confronting Thomas about it. She had made a very nice piece of change from that transaction, if she remembered correctly.

Very quietly she got out of bed and made her way on bare feet to the door. She could hear someone rapping on a door. "Richard, come on!" It was an urgent whisper. "We need to hurry." There was an answering mumble from Richard, and then the sound of his footsteps on the hall carpet.

"Don't see what the rush is," Richard mumbled as their muffled footsteps receded down the hall. Kitty opened her door a crack, but couldn't see anything. Quickly she went into the hall, clad only in her nightrail, and went down toward the back steps. She could hear Richard and Thomas making their way cautiously down the dark stairs, Richard making muffled curses as he kept banging into the wall in the dark.

"Will you keep quiet!" Thomas hissed.

"How do you expect me to keep quiet when I keep knocking my head into this damned wall?" Richard sputtered. "At least you know where you're going. Or you're supposed to, at any rate. He was rewarded by another "Ssshhh!" from Thomas. The noise ceased as Kitty heard the sound of the back door being opened, then quietly shut behind them.

She turned and sped back into her room and watched from the window, taking care to hide behind the curtain. It would be just like Thomas to look up to see if she had heard anything and was watching. Tonight, however, he seemed caught up in his journey, as he hurried Richard around the house where they came into view. As Kitty had thought they would, they turned down the path towards the beach and were out of sight in just a moment.

Quickly Kitty put on her old dark gown and her sturdy shoes. No more freezing behind a bush, she promised herself. She put on her warmest cloak, which fortunately was a dark navy. It did have shiny gold buttons, but there was nothing she could do about that right now. She had to hurry if she was to catch up with Richard and Thomas and find out what they were about.

It had taken her longer than she realized to dress, and when she topped the crest of the cliff leading down to the beach, she saw no trace of the two. She went cautiously down the path, afraid that they might be on the beach somewhere, and a loose rock or a crunch of shingle might alert them to her presence. It took her almost forty-five minutes to make what would ordinarily be a leisurely stroll of twenty minutes or so. Finally, after what seemed an eternity to her, she was down on the beach. A long, careful look up and down assured her that Thomas and Richard were nowhere to be seen along the edge of the sea. That left only two possibilities: either they had taken the sea path to Sherbourne, which seemed unlikely, or they were on board the *Erinys*.

Since she didn't know if there were any of the crew aboard, Kitty was more than careful as she boarded the boat. Every creak of the gangplank made her pause and hold her breath, terrified that she would be discovered. She didn't worry so much about Richard or Thomas finding her as she did that some of the crew would discover her presence. She could manage Richard or Thomas quite easily, but Montfort's crew, or Montfort himself, would be an animal of a different stripe.

Finally she gained the deck, and slipped around to the side. She could hear voices coming from the cabin, and there was a square of light shining on the deck from the lantern that lit the interior. She could smell tobacco smoke, pungent on the sea air, and hear the voices laughing and talking. It sounded like a party of some sort. Carefully, slowly, she picked her way across the deck and came up against the side of the cabin, trying to blend into the shadows. The gold buttons on her cloak glittered in the moonlight, and she tried to cover them with her hands. It wouldn't do to be discovered.

At last she was near the window. She couldn't remember how clean it was, but she had hoped it would be grimy so she could peer in unobserved. Curse Montfort, it was as spotless as the rest of the *Erinys*. She kept to one side, risking a quick look through the very edge of the pane. The inside of the cabin itself was a smoky haze, and she couldn't see very much except some men sitting around a table in the middle of the floor. She didn't dare look longer. She withdrew to the side of the window and tried to listen. The voices were a jumble, but then she began to sort them out. There was Montfort's, of course, and Richard's, and some others she couldn't identify; now she was almost able to decipher what they were saying. She moved closer to the windowpane, planning to risk another look.

Suddenly, roughly, she was seized from behind. She started to scream, but a hand was clamped firmly over her mouth, and she was dragged away from the window. She tried to plant her feet firmly onto the decking to make it as difficult as possible for her assailant. She bent and twisted, trying to get away from the grasp that held her, but whoever it was was much stronger than she. She tried again to scream, making a muffled sound under the hand over her mouth. Then he spoke in her ear. "For God's sake, Kitty, do be quiet! It's me, Thomas!"

Kitty went limp as he half dragged her, and she half stumbled across the deck, her feet making a rasping sound as they dragged across the decking. He still held her, closely and almost cruelly, hand across her mouth. She didn't resist as he held her and dragged her down the gangplank. It was not until they were well onto the beach that he moved his hand from her mouth. "Not a sound," he warned, in a voice that was quite unlike Thomas. Kitty decided to be silent.

He gave her a small push, and they walked swiftly up the path until they were out of sight of the boat, Thomas holding onto her arm all the while. "I'm not going to run away, Thomas," she said indignantly, but he didn't loosen his hold. Finally they reached the crest of the cliff and came to Kitty's favorite spot. Thomas stopped abruptly and sat her down, not too gently, on a rock. "Now, Miss, perhaps you'll tell me what you're doing?"

Kitty was enraged. "*Me* tell you?" She stood up and stared at him in the moonlight. "Perhaps *you* should be explaining things to me, Thomas. You seem to be the one who's in over his head."

"What are you talking about?" He was trying not to yell, and it was an obvious effort for him to keep his voice down. "Don't you know that your reputation would be in shreds right now if anyone except me had found you skulking around a boat full of men in the middle of the night. Just what were you trying to prove?"

Kitty glared at him and her voice was icy. "I happen to be as aware of the proprieties as you are, Thomas, and I realize what might have happened."

Actually, she had thought about the possibility, but hadn't really considered the consequences until that awful moment when a hand clamped over her mouth. However, she would die before she would admit as much to Thomas. "As far as what I was trying to prove, since you don't seem to want to prove your innocence, or Montfort's for that matter, perhaps you should consider that I was trying to save you from making a total ruin of your life."

"*My* life!" It was almost a screech. Thomas took a deep breath and got himself under control. "Whatever are you talking about?"

"The smuggling, Thomas. That's what I'm talking about."

He looked at her incredulously. "Are you still beating that dead horse? I told you it was all stuff and nonsense, and you won't listen. You're making a complete cake out of yourself."

Kitty stared at him. "I saw you, Thomas," she said slowly, standing up to face him, then stood looking out to sea.

"You saw me? Doing what? When?" He sat beside her. "I don't know what you're talking about, Kit."

She looked at him in the moonlight. "I think you do, Thomas. I followed you the other night and I saw you. Richard wasn't with you, but you and Montfort were talking with two men. I heard the two of you make arrangements with those two thieves and even saw Montfort give them some money."

"Kitty, you're daft. It's too many novels again." He chuckled.

"That banter won't work this time, Thomas. I'm telling you I was there. The men were named Williams and Jacques. I saw and heard them."

The names stopped Thomas. "Oh, my God," he said, horrified. He ran his hands through his hair.

"Am I the unexpected something, somewhere that Montfort feared might go wrong?" she asked. "I heard him say that something always did."

"Oh, my God, yes. Kit, for God's sake, why do you have to be so nosy? Things were going along so smoothly."

"I wasn't nosy. I'm just trying to help you or, rather, to save you. Thomas, do you have any idea what it would do to Maman and Papa if you were disgraced by being caught smuggling? How could you have forgotten what you owe your family." She paused and looked intently at his face, shadowy and pale in the moonlight. "It's Montfort's influence, isn't it? That's what has addled you until you can't think straight. Well, Thomas, I can't believe you would let Montfort drag you down that far." Her voice broke.

Thomas picked up her hand. "Kit, I swear it's not that. Montfort doesn't have anything to do with this." He stopped and amended his statement as Kitty stared at him. "All right, he is involved, but I can't say anything about it right now. Can't you trust me a little bit? Please? Remember I did promise to tell you everything as soon as I honorably could. I swear I will." He smiled at her, but it had no effect on Kitty

"No, Thomas. I can't trust you in this. You're going to have to tell Montfort that you want out, because if you don't, I will. I won't have the family disgraced. It would kill Papa."

Thomas dropped her hand. "I can't get out right now. It ain't exactly that way," he said slowly.

"What do you mean?"

He looked at her and gave her his slow, lazy

smile. "I mean, dear little sister, that Montfort's in with me, not the other way around."

Kitty was aghast. "I don't believe it, Thomas," she finally said. "You're not that sort, and I know that better than anyone. I know you'd do whatever had to be done—even give your life—for England if need be. You'd never be the one who'd get into any kind of illegal trade."

He smiled again, a twisted smile this time. "Gambling debts can make a man do things he never dreamed of, Kitty."

"Thomas," she implored, "we could do something about your debts. There's no need for you to get mixed up in something that might disgrace you or the family. You could even be hanged!" Her voice quivered.

Thomas put an arm around her shaking shoulders. "Now, Kit, don't be so melodramatic. Nothing's going to happen to me, and no one is going to know. Believe me, if you'll just keep quiet for a few days, this will all be over. I'll have my blunt, Montfort will have his, and no one will be the wiser."

"Someone could find out, Thomas. After all, *I* found out, didn't I?"

He laughed. "Yes, but you always find out everything. No one else cares what happens along this stretch of the coast."

"We could pay your debts, Thomas. I'll give you my quarter's allowance."

He squeezed her shoulders. "That's sweet of you, Kit, but I'm afraid your quarter's allowance wouldn't make a dent in what I owe. Just keep quiet, that's all I ask. Things will be solved in jig time."

Kitty sat, lost in thought. It was so unlike Thomas. "It's Montfort, isn't it?" she asked slowly. "He's forced you to gamble and gotten you into debt until he can make you do what he wants."

"That's ridiculous!" He sat down beside her and dropped his hands to his lap, but he didn't look at Kitty. "I've told you again and again that Montfort's one of the best men I've ever met. If you knew him the way I do, you'd think so as well."

Kitty remembered wistfully. "I admit I disliked him at the beginning, but after we talked, especially the day the Montforts and Harriette Marlowe caught me in my cleaning clothes, I was well on the way to changing my opinion of him. I only wish . . . ," her voice trailed off.

"You wish what?" There was a hard note underlying Thomas's voice. Kitty had never heard it there before.

"I wish both of us had been right about Montfort. I wish he had been a good, decent man, the kind of man you told me he was, and the kind of man I was beginning to think he was. But Thomas, I know you wouldn't be involved in anything like smuggling on your own. I know you too well. I even know that you gamble, but never to excess."

"This time it was to excess, believe me."

Kitty shook her head. "I'll never believe it, Thomas. The only answer left is Montfort."

"Well, it's the wrong answer," Thomas said shortly, standing up. "I told you that he was helping me, not the other way around."

Kitty stood to face him. "And I don't believe you."

"You'll have to believe what you want. All I ask is a promise from you that you'll keep quiet for a few days or maybe a week or two at the most. Please."

Kitty searched his face in the moonlight and thought about all the years they had shared together. Silence seemed a small thing to do for him,

137

but yet, it rankled. Something was wrong somewhere.

"Well?" Thomas asked.

"I don't know," Kitty answered. "Thomas, I can't let you just throw your whole life away. Just a while ago Maman was talking about you joining government service. You could . . ."

She was interrupted by a short, strange laugh from Thomas. "Government service! Maman has that in mind for me, eh?"

"Yes, and if there's any part of you that's a Walsingham, you'll tell Montfort to take his smuggling and go elsewhere, and then you'll do what Maman and Papa wish you to do."

"Calm down, Kit," Thomas said, looking behind him as if he were being followed. "Come on, let me get you back home."

"So you can go back and gamble some more with Montfort and his bunch of blackguards? That's what they're doing on board the *Erinys*, isn't it?"

Thomas gave her a little push that set her walking beside him. He held her arm tightly. "And what's wrong with that? If you condemned every man in England who had ever gambled, you'd have no one left — including Richard and Papa."

"Richard! You left him back there. You know that Montfort will chop him to little pieces. Thomas, you must go back and rescue him."

Thomas laughed aloud, laughing so hard that he stopped in the middle of the path. "Rescue Richard! My dear poppet, that's a good 'un. Me going off to rescue the coolest hand with a deck of cards this side of London."

"Richard?" Kitty was aghast. "Surely Richard doesn't gamble!"

"Oh, but he does. And what's worse, he always

wins. I've followed him from club to club, trying to learn his secret." Thomas started walking again. "I've watched him time and time again, and I think he always wins because he doesn't care. He doesn't mind to gamble, and if he wins, that's fine; if he loses, that's fine as well. But Richard doesn't really care much for gambling, so you don't need to worry about spending the future standing outside gaol waiting for him."

"Richard?" Kitty was still trying to picture Richard in one gambling hell after another. "You're funning with me, Thomas."

"Swear, Kit." He smiled at her and lifted two fingers as they used to when they were children and promised each other things. "Here we are at the back door. Will you promise to go on up and not come out again tonight?"

"Thomas, you must really reconsider . . ."

He shook his head wearily. "I can see it's going to be a long night. Come on." He opened the door quietly and pushed her through.

"What are you doing?"

"Ssshhh." Thomas closed the door behind them, leaving them in complete darkness. "I'm taking you upstairs, and then I'm staying with you until you go to sleep. I can't take a chance on you straying out again tonight. If it were just me or Richard or Montfort down at the *Erinys,* I might not worry about your reputation, but there are a couple of high flyers down there who might put a word or two in the wrong places. So, dear Kit, I intend to stay right here and watch you." He pushed her up the stairs and onto the carpeted hallway. "If the mountain won't come to Mohamet, or some such saying."

"This is ridiculous," Kitty muttered as Thomas

gave her another little shove into her chamber and closed the door behind them.

"I heartily agree," he said. "If I could extract a promise from you, and if I could trust you, this would be quite unnecessary."

"What will you tell the others? Surely they'll miss you."

Thomas lit her candle and gave her an engaging grin. "I'll give them some kind of Banbury tale about meeting one of the village girls on the beach. I'm quite sure they'll believe me."

"Quite." Kit bit the word off. She glared at Thomas as he took off his close fitting coat of maroon superfine, unbuttoned his waistcoat, and settled down, sprawling comfortably all over her boudoir chair.

"Don't mind me," he said, grinning. "I'll be perfectly comfortable right here. You go right on to bed as usual. Just leave the candle burning so I can see you."

Kit sat on the edge of the bed. "Thomas, I still don't believe you."

He opened his eyes. "About what?"

"About Montfort. About you being involved in the smuggling to pay off gambling debts. It doesn't ring true."

"Of course it does. Go to sleep." He settled over to one side of the chair and closed his eyes. Kitty waited for fifteen minutes, waiting for him to go to sleep, then she got up and went across the room. Without warning, he reached out and grabbed her wrist. "Going somewhere, Kit?"

She went back and sat on the edge of the bed. "Just testing you, Thomas."

"I thought as much," he said with a chuckle. "Now go back to bed and get some sleep. Don't want you looking a fright tomorrow. Maman will be sure to ask if you're coming down with something."

Kitty looked at him. "Thomas."

"Uuummm."

"Thomas, if you want to go back to the *Erinys,* or if you want to go to bed, I promise I'll stay here for the night." She held up two fingers in the familiar gesture. "Swear."

"Ah, Kit, if I could only trust you." He stretched, obviously as stiff and uncomfortable as he had looked.

"No, I mean it, I promise. The only thing I ask is that we talk more about this tomorrow."

"There's nothing more to say, Kit."

She crawled into bed, dark dress and all. "I promise, Thomas."

"Uuummm. Goodnight, Kit," he said, attempting one more time to get comfortable in the chair. He sat there for a while watching her from half-closed eyes until he was sure she was asleep, then blew out the candle and left. However, since he knew Kit so well, he took the precaution of locking her chamber door as he went out.

Chapter Thirteen

Kitty was awakened the next morning by Bidwell beating on her door. She sat up in bed, wondered briefly why she had gone to bed in her dark dress, and then remembered the night before. "Drat that Thomas," she muttered as she fell out of bed and made her way to the door.

"What do you want?" she yelled to Bidwell. The door seemed to be locked, and she couldn't find the key.

"Are you all right?"

"Of course I'm all right," she answered, down on hands and knees looking for the key. "I can't find the key."

"It's out here, on the outside," Bidwell said.

Kitty stood. "Bidwell, I didn't know you were such a goose. If the key's out there, open the door."

The lock scraped and Bidwell flung the door open dramatically, barely missing Kitty who jumped back at the last minute. "I thought something was wrong!" Bidwell announced, standing in the doorway.

"Nothing is wrong except I haven't had my chocolate," Kitty grumbled, noticing Bidwell's astonishment at seeing her in the dark, thoroughly wrinkled, dress. "I need to change into something fresher, Bidwell," she said, sitting down in her boudoir chair. "Perhaps you might try my hair in curls on top as well," she suggested, knowing that nothing in the world could distract Bidwell more than a chance to deck her lady out to the nines. The ploy worked, for an hour later, a well-dressed, but thoroughly ravenous Kitty made her way downstairs. Bidwell had forgotten everything except rigging her out in a cherry and white striped dress with white ribands. Bunches of artificial cherries Grand-mère had purchased in Quimper decorated the hem, and a bunch was placed in the curls of her hair. Kitty felt absolutely ridiculous, but Bidwell proclaimed her the height of fashion. Bidwell also, after admiring her finished product, did remember to ask Kitty why she felt it necessary to be dressed so for a morning in the country. Kitty, never much of a liar, had to make up something, and the best she could do on short notice was to tell Bidwell that Maman had asked her to make a trip into the village. Bidwell raised an expressive eyebrow at this falsehood, but said nothing.

When Kitty got down to the breakfast room, Thomas was just finishing up. He asked the same question, received the same answer, and laughed thoroughly. "Couldn't come up with anything else, eh, Kit?"

"I didn't have time to think of something cleverer," she snapped, then grinned at him. "I had to do something to keep Bidwell from asking why I had spent the night in my dark dress." She stopped and looked at her brother. "Don't think you've gammoned me, Thomas. I haven't forgotten what we discussed last night, and I intend to talk to you about it later."

He flushed guiltily. "Just give me some time, Kit. Please." He looked at her earnestly. "I'll explain everything, I promise."

"Would you like to walk to the village with me this morning and explain then? I'd be glad to listen as we walked." Kit poured another cup of chocolate and buttered another muffin. She was extremely hungry.

Thomas shook his head. "No, I have something else to do."

"And what does Montfort have in mind for you today?" she asked with sarcasm. "Thomas, you must . . ."

He stood abruptly. "I told you before, Kit, that Montfort was in with me, not the other way around. I don't want to hear any more about it. I'll tell you when the time is right and not before." He strode out of the breakfast room, leaving Kitty sipping her cup of chocolate. Perhaps Maman was right about Thomas. He seemed to be changing right under Kitty's very eyes. She didn't know what to think of him lately. He wasn't at all the same.

Midmorning found Kitty walking the road to the village. It was almost always a nice walk, and Kitty usually enjoyed it immensely. The road followed the edge of the sea, and she loved to walk along it and see the rocks on the edge of the water, watching the surf break against them. Then too, it was always a mystical feeling to look across into the clouds and know that France was there, just beyond the horizon. Today, however, she saw nothing as she walked. She spent the time worrying about the events of the past days. The problem of Thomas and Montfort kept bothering her. It was as though something important, something she couldn't place, was nagging right at the edge of her consciousness, but she couldn't seem to put a name to it. She knew if she could just put that piece of the puzzle into place, everything else would be solved.

For one thing, she kept trying to categorize Montfort's character and came up with another facet each time. Was he the sinner, the sinned with, or the sinned against? Kitty couldn't place him. By the time she reached the village, she still hadn't come up with any answers, but she had managed to run right into Mrs. Braithwaite and her Barbara outside the inn.

"And how is your family?" Mrs. Braithwaite asked, with a touch of too much friendliness.

"Fine," Kitty answered. "How are you, Barbara?"

Barbara stared miserably at the ground, her face flaming red with embarrassment. When she failed to say anything, her mother prompted her. "Barbara is doing fine, thank you. Say something, Barbara."

"How are you?" mumbled Barbara.

Her mother glared sharply at her. "My dear Miss Walsingham, you simply must come over to our house and give my poor Barbara the benefit of your experience. I know you've already had something of a season in London, and know simply everyone there."

"I wouldn't say that," Kitty began, but Mrs. Braithwaite overrode her.

"My dear Barbara is planning a London season, you know. I'm sure she'll be the toast of the *ton*, but I know she would love for you to come over and give her some pointers." Mrs. Braithwaite gave Kitty a wink and a hideous conspiratorial smile. "Such things as how to handle a beau, or how to reject a proposal gracefully."

"Please, Mama," Barbara managed to say.

Mrs. Braithwaite patted her hand. "Now, Barbara, you know how much you admire Miss Walsingham." She turned back to Kitty. "Perhaps,

Miss Walsingham, when you come over to visit, you might bring your brother with you. He's always been a favorite of mine."

"Please, Mama." It was Barbara again, speaking in a strangled voice. "We really must go."

Kitty felt compassion for Barbara, a plain girl who had always been manipulated by the social passions of her father and mother. "Perhaps Barbara could come by Bellevoir one day," she said, knowing she would regret it. "I'm sure we could find several things to talk about."

Mrs. Braithwaite beamed. "We shall certainly do that. I do want to thank you for your interest in my darling daughter." Mrs. Braithwaite smiled coyly. "Perhaps your brother will be there; I've heard he was home."

"I'm sure Thomas would be delighted to see Barbara and you," Kitty said. It was a complete lie, but necessary. Barbara's face lit up and for the first time, she looked at Kitty.

"Delighted?" She said the word breathlessly, and Kitty instantly wished she hadn't used the word. She had given Barbara hope where none existed.

"I'm sure he'll be delighted," Mrs. Braithwaite said. "We'll be over soon, Miss Walsingham." With that, the Braithwaites went on down the street, Barbara so excited that her feet scarcely seemed to touch the ground.

Kitty went on about her errands in the village. Maman had sent some calves-foot jelly to the vicar's wife and had asked Kitty to post a letter for her. It was addressed to some close friends in London, and Kitty guessed that Maman, in her usual efficient way, was wasting no time in inquiring about a government post for Thomas. Kitty also went to the local mantua-maker to ask about some green ribands that were to match her green sarsnet. It was right outside Miss Dumbarton's establishment that she ran into Harriette Marlowe.

"My dear Miss Walsingham," Harriette trilled. "How delighted I am to see you! I mentioned only this morning to Marianne and James that I hoped to see you again soon."

Kitty lifted an eyebrow at the mention of "Marianne and James," but Harriette went right on. "Won't you come have some refreshment with me at the Dolphin Inn? I have already bespoke a private parlor so I could have a cup of tea, so now we can have a comfortable cose. I would dearly love the company." Again Kitty looked at her. It was impossible to read Harriette's expressions.

"I must be getting back," Kitty began, but Harriette spoke again.

"Oh, please. Just a quick cup of tea. It will do both of us a world of good, and there are some things I do want to confide to you."

Kitty couldn't imagine whatever Harriette would wish to confide to *her*, and went on to the Dolphin, in part because she couldn't think of a plausible excuse, in part because she was curious.

Mrs. Waggoner settled them into a cozy private parlor overlooking the sea and brought them their tea and some cakes. As soon as the landlady left them alone, Harriette turned to Kitty, waving a delicately scented envelope. "My dear, I am just bursting with news, and I can't wait to tell it!"

"Really?" Kitty was faintly uneasy.

Harriette went on, oblivious to any undercurrent. "Yes, Miss Walsingham, I am writing my dear papa today to let him know that an announcement for the papers can be prepared."

"An announcement?"

"Yes! Isn't it wonderful?" Harriette was looking fondly at the envelope and smiling broadly. "Papa will be overjoyed." She looked at Kitty. "As you know, there has been something of an understanding between James and myself."

Kitty felt as if the ground had dropped out from under her feet, and was silently thankful that she was sitting down. "Am I to take it that you and Captain Montfort . . . ?"

"Yes, dear Miss Walsingham! Yes! I am telling Papa to prepare the announcement for the *Courier.* I must go up to London directly and begin wedding preparations. James, of course, will want nothing except the finest." She looked at Kitty with a smile that Kitty couldn't read. "Perhaps we could do some shopping together. After all, we'll both be buying much the same thing—wedding dresses and trousseaux. Are you all right, Miss Walsingham?" she asked as Kitty choked on a piece of cake and had to gulp down her tea.

Kitty wiped at her eyes. "I'm quite fine, thank you. Please allow me to wish you and Captain Montfort every happiness."

"Thank you." Harriette's smile could only be described as triumphant. "I'm sure we shall be quite happy. James, of course, will have to forget this quaint notion he has of living in the country. One of the first things I intend to have him purchase is a more fashionable town house." She waved the envelope again to emphasize her point. "He says he doesn't want one; however, once we're married, I'm quite sure I'll be able to change his mind on those matters."

"I'm quite sure." Kitty's response was automatic.

Harriette tapped the corner of the envelope against the table. "After all, I believe James only has those maggoty thoughts about how wonderful the country is because he's been away. Do you know what he told me?" Here Harriette lowered her voice conspiratorially. "He disliked Paris! Can you imagine? I've always wanted to travel—Paris, Florence, Rome."

"Perhaps the captain will change his mind." Kitty was speaking through stiff lips. She hoped Harriette didn't notice.

"Oh, quite right. I'm sure he'll love travelling as much as I, and as for living in town, I think I merely need to get myself—and him, of course—set in society, and he will be quite happy there. After all, he'll have a club. Perhaps several."

"Yes, Thomas seems to find them very time-consuming," Kitty said, seeing Montfort wasting all his time dallying around the clubs, gambling and drinking away the day with friends as so many of the dandies did. Even worse was the thought of seeing Montfort shackled to a social butterfly like Harriette. The picture wasn't pleasant; the man would chafe at the bit after less than a season. Harriette obviously didn't know him very well. Or didn't want to.

"Don't you think so, Miss Walsingham?" Harriette's voice drew Kitty back to the present.

"Yes, of course," Kitty said, having no idea what Harriette was asking. Then, seeing that Harriette obviously expected some comment on whatever she had said, Kitty confessed, "I'm sorry, I was woolgathering. What did you say?"

Harriette gave her an arch look. "I was saying, Miss Walsingham, that all it ever takes to bring a man up to scratch is a firm hand. I'm sure you found that true with Lord Richard."

"Up to scratch?" Kitty wasn't at all sure what

Harriette had in mind. "Whatever do you mean?"

"Oh, come now," Harriette said, rising impatiently. "I know very well that you coerced Lord Richard into proposing, and I applaud you for it. After all, as females, we all use the same methods."

Kitty felt her cheeks burn. "Coerced," she screeched, ready to ring a peal over the incomparable Miss Marlowe, but that lady cut her short before she could utter a word.

"Of course, coerced. Don't we all? Dear Miss Walsingham, if we didn't give these worthy gentlemen a good assist, we'd all sit on the shelf forever. Believe me, every woman employs these tactics."

"I want you to know . . . ," Kitty began, but Harriette interrupted her.

"I fully understand your position, Miss Walsingham, and I assure you that your secret is safe with me. After all, I've done the same thing." Harriette swept to the door of the parlor. "Good day, Miss Walsingham. I've enjoyed our chat immensely, but I really must run and get this letter posted to Papa. I know he's anxious to receive it." With that, she strode out of the parlor, leaving Kitty sitting there seething with rage.

"Coerced, indeed," Kitty muttered, staring white-lipped at the door of the parlor. "I imagine if anyone in this world was ever coerced, it was Captain Montfort." She looked over at Harriette's empty chair as a strange, empty feeling settled in the pit of her stomach. "Poor Montfort," she said involuntarily.

Kitty was still feeling a conflict of emotions when she left the Dolphin. On one hand, she pitied Montfort for being saddled with someone like Harriette for a lifetime. On the other hand, she thought it served him well for being the scoundrel who had dragged Thomas into gambling. No matter what Thomas said, Kitty knew Montfort was at fault somewhere. Added to all these feelings was a strong dose of pure rage at the high-handed manner of Harriette Marlowe. Coerced, indeed!

Kitty decided to dispel part of her anger by walking the long way back home, taking the wagon road, then veering off along the edge of the beach. The tide was out and the sand was packed hard, so her slippers would not suffer, and her clothing wouldn't get wet from the surf. She walked rapidly, enjoying the soothing feel of the sea wind against her skin. As she walked, she thought of hundreds of *bon mots* and pithy remarks she could have made to Harriette, but now she would never have the chance. It always seemed to happen to her that way.

She had calmed down by the time she got to the path leading up to Bellevoir, and stopped there to take a long look across the Channel. The *Erinys* was moored at the dock, spotless and gleaming white against the sparkling water, riding low since the tide was out. The longer Kitty stared at the boat, the more convinced she was that there was some clue there that she was missing, one thing that might perhaps either clear Thomas completely or else convince him to give up his involvement in the smuggling scheme.

Kitty took a quick look around, even walking part of the way up towards Sherbourne. Seeing no one, either on the path or the deserted beach, she decided now was the best time to do some investigating on her own. She hadn't promised Thomas she wouldn't investigate, and she might find something that would free him, something that would prove that he, and perhaps even Montfort, were pawns of someone else. Before she could change her mind, she anchored her parcel underneath a rock beside the path to Bellevoir and then walked rapidly across the beach to the boat, her slippers making soft crunching sounds on the smooth, hard-packed sand.

Looking behind her, Kitty could see her tracks plainly in the sand. Anyone coming down to the beach would know that someone had visited the boat. She paused. Perhaps no one would come down until the tide came back in and washed them away. It was a chance she was going to have to take. It was too late for her to stop now. Pausing again, but hearing nothing, she made her way up the gangplank and onto the polished deck of the *Erinys*.

Slowly Kitty walked across the deck towards the cabin. She felt exactly like what she was—an intruder. She kept reminding herself that she was doing this for Thomas. She *had* to find something.

The cabin window was still spotless, and Kitty looked in. To her surprise, she saw various papers on the table in the middle, stacked neatly into piles. Through the window she could see the cabin door across on the other side of the cabin. It looked as if it were unlatched. She was surprised a man as methodical and tidy as Montfort would leave it that way, but perhaps he had been in a hurry. As it was, she knew she had to look through those papers, no matter what the risk. She could count Montfort's oversight as her good fortune.

Slowly, carefully, she made her way around the sides of the cabin, mentally laughing at herself for being so careful when it was obvious there was no one around. At the edge of the cabin corner, she stopped, suddenly hearing a distinct hum. She stood still, trying to place the sound when it hit her that it was a man, humming softly to himself. She caught her breath before she dared look around the edge of the cabin, and when she looked, she froze.

Montfort was there, down on his hands and knees on the deck where she hadn't been able to see him from the beach. He seemed to be measuring something, working on it with something sharp, a knife or some kind of awl. Kitty took in these details automatically. But there were details that took longer to register. Montfort had been working for a while and had removed his shirt, casually tossing it over a nearby railing. He was bent, back to her, and Kitty stared at him, his back tanned and smooth, glistening with sweat as the sun beat down on him. His hair glinted almost gold in the sunlight, and he hummed to himself as he worked. On his right side was the evidence of one of his war wounds — a ragged white scar wrapping around his side that slashed through the olive of his skin like a lightning flash. Kitty had to fight down an impulse to reach out and touch him.

She felt dizzy and weak and leaned against the side of the cabin for support. The boards creaked only slightly, but Montfort leaped to his feet, quickly grabbing up a short-bladed knife that lay beside him. In one smooth motion, he turned, balancing on the balls of his feet, his knife in his hand as he advanced towards her, the blade upraised. Kitty cringed against the side of the painted boards, trying to make herself invisible.

Slowly, carefully, Montfort brought the knife down. "I'm sorry, Miss Walsingham," he said smoothly, as though a visit from her was commonplace, and he usually greeted visitors with a knife in hand. He was so close that Kitty could see beads of sweat roll slowly down the dark golden hairs on his chest and smell the faintly musky smell of him. He came even closer to her and took her hand. She looked up at him and started to say something, but words never came. He came closer and closer, almost, but not quite touching her, a strange look in his amber eyes. From a distance, Kitty heard the sound of the knife hitting the deck. Then, slowly, almost cautiously, he touched the side of her face with his fingertips. Kitty looked up at him, forgetting everything except the strange warmth in his eyes, the sudden rush of emotion his nearness caused. His fingertips slid along her cheek, and he put his other hand behind her neck. Before she knew what was happening, he had drawn her close to him, and his mouth was on hers, soft and exploring.

Kitty leaned into him and reveled in the sensations—the touch of stubble on his face gently rubbing her skin, the taste of salty sweat on his lips as they moved over hers, the sharp, masculine smell of his body, the dampness of his chest against hers. She reached out to him, her fingers slowly sliding up his smooth, sweaty back, gently slipping over the ridges of the scar and moving up to his neck, where her fingers locked together in the gold tipped tendrils of his hair. He pulled back and looked at her, not speaking, and his eyes were so dark that Kitty felt she was almost drowning in them. He must have seen an answering look in hers as he bent and kissed her again, not as tentatively this time. Kitty's body seemed to be falling and flying at the same time as she moved closer against him, wanting to be a part of him.

Again he pulled away slightly, looking at her. This time, however, the dark, unreadable look in his eyes quickly faded, replaced by the slightly mocking look she had seen the first time they met. His body stiffened as he moved away from her. "Well, Miss Walsingham, I suppose Richard will be forced to call me out for this breach of manners."

Kitty didn't answer him. She was unable to speak. He looked at her again, a mocking smile on his face. "However, I suppose you and I might want to keep this a secret. I assure you it will never happen again. A momentary slip on my part."

"No doubt you mistook me for Miss Marlowe," Kitty snapped, infuriated by his mocking tone. Evidently her kisses had not inspired the same emotions in him that he had given to her. Even now she felt slightly dizzy. She moved back to lean against the cabin wall for support.

"No need to try to run away, Miss Walsingham. I assure you that I'm perfectly harmless. You have my word on it." There was an undertone of laughter in his voice.

"I'm not worried," Kitty said stiffly, watching every move he made as he went to the railing and picked up his shirt, the muscles in his back and shoulders rippling as he moved. He casually put the shirt on, tying the neck loosely. The linen of the shirt immediately clung to his damp body, outlining it. Kitty heard him chuckle and looked up into his eyes. She realized he had been watching her look at him, and she blushed furiously.

Montfort was still laughing as he bent to pick up his knife. "I suppose I should put this out of your reach," he said. "From what your brother tells me, you might be tempted to use it." He took the knife over to where he had been working and placed it carefully under a pile of rags. Kitty wondered for a moment why he was hiding it, but his next sentence distracted her. "As for mistaking you for Miss

Marlowe—no, Miss Walsingham, there's no way I could possibly do that."

Visions of Harriette's perfect blonde beauty floated in front of Kitty, and she stiffened. "I think I understand, Captain Montfort," she said, trying not to let any emotion show in her voice. It was perfectly obvious to her that there was no way he could mistake someone like her for an incomparable like Harriette.

"I hope you do, Miss Walsingham," he said softly, giving her a strange look.

"I do." She drew herself up and stared icily at him. "I only meant that you were thinking of Miss Marlowe since she has let me in on your secret."

"My secret?"

Kitty tried to read the look on his face, but he seemed only puzzled. "Yes. Miss Marlowe was preparing the announcement and posting it to her father. I wish the two of you very happy."

"The deuce!"

Kitty backed away from him. "It's quite all right, Captain Montfort. Miss Marlowe gave me to understand that this is not public knowledge yet, so your secret is safe with me."

He gave her a small, mocking bow. "Delighted to hear that, Miss Walsingham. I hope all my secrets are as safe."

"As a matter of fact, Captain Montfort, . . ." Kitty began, summoning up her courage to ask him about Thomas and the strange scene she had witnessed. Montfort must have sensed what she was going to say because he interrupted her.

"May I escort you back home, Miss Walsingham?" He came toward her, kicking part of whatever he had been working on aside. "I'm afraid you might get too much of this hot sun out here without your bonnet. I'm sure Richard wouldn't want a beet-red bride." The mocking grin became wider.

"Don't trouble yourself," Kitty said stiffly, turning to go since he had so rudely dismissed her. Then she stopped and faced him, trying to sound calm. "Captain Montfort, I wish to speak with you about a matter of some importance. About Thomas and . . ."

His mocking amber eyes looked right through her. "I regret I have another appointment right now, Miss Walsingham, but I'd be delighted to speak with you at any other time."

"Tomorrow, then." Kitty was insistent.

The mocking look faded, replaced by a strange, dark look Kitty couldn't read. "Very well, Miss Walsingham, tomorrow. Would you like me to call on you?"

"No, I'll come here."

The mocking look and tone returned. "On the *Erinys?* Delighted, Miss Walsingham, but I do have one small request." Kitty had turned and crossed the deck to leave, but looked back at him.

"I suggest you bring your abigail, Miss Walsingham," he said with a chuckle.

"My abigail?"

Montfort leaned negligently against the railing, his body clearly outlined by his damp shirt clinging to it. "I don't think either Lord Richard or Miss Marlowe would care for a repeat performance of, ah, our interlude, however much I might look forward to it."

Kitty's face flamed as she turned and left without answering him. As she walked across the beach and toward the path, she could hear him still chuckling.

Chapter Fourteen

Kitty had gotten all the way home and shut her chamber door behind her before she remembered her parcel, still carefully anchored underneath a rock at the foot of the path. She thought for a moment of sending Bidwell or one of the footmen to fetch it, but discarded the idea. She had already done enough retreating before the enemy. Finding a bonnet, she put it on and went back out and down the path, although very carefully, watching for Montfort. When she approached the bend in the path where she could see the *Erinys*, but could not yet be seen, she paused and looked. Someone else was there with Montfort, a slight, very stylishly dressed gentleman. They were standing on the beach in front of the boat, talking. Kitty stood for a moment wondering who the man might be. There was no doubt about his status—something in the way he dressed and carried himself proclaimed him to be a gentleman. She even briefly considered trying to get nearer to see, or even walking brazenly up the beach. Montfort would then be forced to introduce her to his companion.

She hesitated, looked again at the two talking, then decided that there was a time for valor and a time to be prudent. With a careful turn, she went back home and sent the downstairs footman back for her ribands.

Kitty spent the remainder of the day worrying about her coming interview with Montfort. Would he really be there to talk to her? Should she take Bidwell with her? Her face burned as she remembered what had happened on the boat and how she had felt. He probably thought her something of a lightskirt, letting men kiss her like that. She alternated between anguish and a delight in remembering her feelings. She had never been kissed like that before, but she knew she wanted to be kissed that way again, and yet again.

Kitty dressed for dinner with care. She let Bidwell get out her good jonquil sarsnet with the white underslip. Her new ribands matched perfectly, and Bidwell wove them through her hair, pulling one down around her face to fall to her shoulders along with her curls. Kitty looked in the glass at herself with satisfaction. "Very good, Bidwell," she said with a smile. Bidwell wouldn't allow herself to show satisfaction beyond a smug "I know."

Richard and Thomas were already downstairs. "Lord, you look smashing, Kit," Thomas said, surveying her through his quizzing glass. "Turning into a regular looker in your old age."

"And you're turning to senility in your old age," she said, looking right back at him. He had on a new waistcoat of a particularly vile shade of green. "Where did you find *that?*" she asked, pointing to his waistcoat. "Did you have that dyed with pond scum?"

Thomas managed to look offended. "Pond scum? I'll have you know that this color is all the crack." He looked down at the waistcoat in question. "I do admit that this color looked somewhat better on the bolt. I thought I'd give it a trial run here in the country."

"I believe you'd better retire it before you go to town. The *ton* will cut you dead if you appear in that."

Thomas shook his head. "Wager you ten pounds that I could start a new trend with this."

"You're on," said Richard quickly. "Within two months."

They were interrupted by Maman coming down the stairs. "Just what are you children talking about?" She stopped and stared. "Thomas, wherever did you find that atrocious waistcoat?"

Thomas looked offended while Richard laughed, asking if Thomas wished to pay up immediately. Thomas ignored him, and as Papa came in, they all went in to supper.

After supper, they went to the drawing room and played cards while Papa sat smoking his pipe, watching them. Finally, Papa excused himself, pleading an early day on the morrow, and Maman went upstairs to read. The three left were too few to play cards, and Thomas didn't want to do anything else. He seemed quite out of sorts, and Kitty guessed the cause was his waistcoat. The green seemed to grow more hideous by the hour. With much grumbling Thomas decided to settle himself in with a book, but before fifteen minutes were out, he was snoring peacefully on the sofa.

"I believe the country is getting to Thomas," Kitty said to Richard. "In town, he'd be up until daylight."

"He's been getting up early," Richard said.

"Really? What for?" Kitty was instantly interested.

Richard looked at her. "No reason," he said, quite obviously lying. His face was red and he couldn't look at Kitty.

Kitty tried but could get no more out of him. She

got up and walked to the window, looking out at the moon hanging near a cloud over the Channel. "Would you like to go with me for a walk outside, Richard?" she asked suddenly. There was something she *had* to find out.

"Now?"

Kitty walked over and took his hand. "Of course now. It's a beautiful night outside. Why don't we go out and look at the moon?"

Richard looked doubtful. "We can see it just fine from the window," he said.

Kitty stared at him in complete exasperation. "I would like very much to walk in the garden, Richard."

"Good God, Kit, there's going to be a fog coming in, and you'll catch your death out there. Why don't we play cards now that Thomas is asleep? Two hands."

"I have a shawl, Richard, and I'm going outside. Do you wish to accompany me?" Kitty started for the door, only to be stopped by Thomas's voice.

"Richard, will you give in gracefully and take that termagant outside? How ever can I get any rest if I'm forever having to listen to her whine?"

Kitty turned on the recumbent form. "Whine! I have never, never been known to whine. I want you to know, Thomas, that . . ."

Richard, sensing another of their famous disagreements, hurried over to Kitty and dragged her to the door. "Quite right, Kitty."

"What do you mean?" she snapped as she went out the door with Richard's hand pushing her forward. "Do you agree with that sloth in there, that citified dandy who has never had a thought for anyone or anything except the cut of his neckcloth."

"Wrong, wrong," Thomas said, following them out

of the drawing room. "The cut of my neckcloth is quite secondary to the cut of my coat." He grinned broadly at her. "Have a lovely walk in the garden, Kit my pet. I'm off to bed." With that, he bounded up the stairs, leaving Kitty staring after him. Thomas going to bed before midnight! There was only one explanation for such strange behavior on his part, she thought. Thomas must be sick.

Her thoughts were interrupted by Richard speaking in a querulous tone. "Dash it all, Kitty. Are we going to go for a walk in the garden and look at the fog, or are we going to stand here?"

"We're going for a walk in the garden," she said firmly, marching to the door and glaring at Duff as he appeared from nowhere to open the door for them.

Once outside, Kitty calmed down. The breeze from the ocean was cool and salt-tinged, blowing in just a hint of a mist from the sea. It was beautiful to see the moon shining behind a gauzy wisp of sea mist. She led Richard by the box hedge and back towards Maman's pride and joy—the small garden of red and white flowers laid out in a checkerboard pattern. There was a bench there that would be quite satisfactory for Kitty's purpose.

Kitty reached the bench and sat down, leaving room for Richard to sit beside her. He looked at her uncertainly. "Good heavens, Richard, do sit down," she said irritably. Then she remembered her purpose and added sweetly, "Please."

He sat down heavily, not touching her, looking up at the tendrils of mist circling the moon.

"It's beautiful, isn't it?" Kitty asked.

"Going to rain again," Richard said. "Do you want to go back in now? We're both going to catch the ague out here in this fog."

"Richard," Kitty said softly, putting her hand on his arm, and looking up at him with what she hoped was a loving look.

"Uuummm," Richard said, not looking at her. "Probably rain before morning, I'd say."

Kitty tried again. "Richard," she said softly again, exerting a slight pressure on his arm.

"Wonder if we've had much rain at home?" he said absently. "I meant to write and ask. Really, Kit, I'm going to have to go back for a few days. Need to see how everything's going. If there's been much rain, those old drainage tiles won't carry it."

"Richard," she almost shrieked, "will you look at me?"

"Of course, Kit." He turned squarely on the bench to face her. "Did you want something?"

Kitty gave up all pretense of coyness. "Richard," she asked, taking a deep breath, "would you like to kiss me?"

"Well, of course, Kit. Why the deuce didn't you say so?" With that, he leaned over and gave her a peck on the cheek, then straightened up and smiled at her.

Kitty closed her eyes in complete frustration, then looked at Richard. He was looking quite pleased with himself. "Richard, I meant . . . what I meant to say was . . ." She groped for words. "Richard, would you like to kiss me?"

He looked puzzled. "I just did that, Kit."

"No, I mean really *kiss* me. *Really* kiss me."

"Oh." There was a pause while he looked at her, then he glanced warily up at the windows of the house as though looking for someone there. Satisfied that all the windows were dark, he reached out and took both her arms and kissed her soundly on the lips. Kitty leaned into him, waiting for the feeling, but there was nothing. Nothing. She couldn't believe it! It was somewhat how she fancied it would feel to kiss Thomas. There was no dizziness, no feeling of flying, no feeling that this was a beginning of something new and wonderful.

Richard released her and sat up straight. He smiled broadly and, Kitty thought, quite smugly, at her. "Now that was fine," he said.

"Fine," Kitty answered faintly, and Richard seemed quite pleased.

"We should go in now," he said, getting up and extending a hand for Kitty. "I'd like to oblige you in this, but I can't take a chance on catching the ague, and this fog's getting worse."

Kitty went in with him without a word, her mind spinning. She had tried her experiment, but the results were not what she had expected. She had thought Richard's kiss would be much like Montfort's and would leave her with all the same feelings. It hadn't. It hadn't left her with any feeling at all. It had been nothing, but that left her with some other questions—questions she didn't even want to ask, much less answer.

Duff opened the door for them, and Richard led Kitty in by the hand. Kitty could have sworn that Duff winked at Richard, but that was impossible. She looked again, but saw only Duff's impeccably correct, poker face.

Richard walked her to the top of the stairs where she turned to go into her bedchamber. There he stopped and chucked her under the chin, grinning broadly. "Glad to see you're coming around, Kit," he said. "I knew it was only a matter of time. Maybe your grandmère will get here soon, and we can get on with this marriage business. I need to get back to Collingwood Hall soon. I'd like to be there before hunting season starts." With that, he headed off down the hall to his chamber, whistling softly, remembering to do the pretty thing only just before he went in his room. "Goodnight, Kit," he said cheerfully.

In something of a daze, Kitty went into her chamber. Bidwell was there in the dark, but lit a branch of candles when Kitty came in. She was looking quite pleased. Kitty belatedly remembered that someone leaning to one side could see a certain bench in the garden from her window.

She allowed Bidwell to help her undress, listening all the while to Bidwell's drivel about what a wonderful chance it was for Kitty to have a fine young lord like Sir Richard primed and ready to marry her. Bidwell allowed that Sir Richard was a prime 'un, all right, and, pardon her humble opinion, but Kitty was all jingle brains if she didn't snap him up. Kitty was too wrapped up in her mental questions to correct either the cant or the impression.

Kitty came downstairs the next morning, showing all the ravages of a sleepless night. Thomas was already down, looking quite refreshed, and had even finished his breakfast.

"Morning, Kit," he said, taking in her red-rimmed eyes. "Stay up all night planning your trousseau? Richard tells me you're coming around nicely."

"Thomas, I'm warning you . . . ," Kit began, stabbing the air with her fork for emphasis as she filled her plate from the sideboard.

Thomas leaned back in his chair. "Ah, missing your true love, are you? He went out to the stables a while ago, while you were upstairs dreaming about him. Gone to Montfort's."

"I was *not* dreaming about him," Kitty snapped, "and I don't happen to care where he went." Thomas's words sunk in. "Did you say he'd gone to Captain Montfort's?"

"Uuummm." Thomas looked at her with a wicked grin. "Not jealous, are you, Kit? After all, both the sweet Marianne and the delectable Harriette are over there."

"Don't be ridiculous," Kitty said. "Why in the world would Richard go over there at this time of the morning?"

Thomas sighed. "I see you're not going to be jealous, so I might as well confess. He and Montfort are going riding. If it's of any interest to you, I believe Marianne was going along."

"Thomas, that doesn't signify at all." She looked at him. "Why didn't you go? Are you beginning to believe my opinion of Captain Montfort?"

"Not at all." Thomas rose and looked down at her. "I still happen to think him a capital fellow. It's just that I didn't fancy riding at this ungodly hour of the morning."

"I didn't know you fancied riding at any time," Kitty said maliciously.

"Now, Kit. No need to lower yourself to insults," he said. "It's just that I really should be abed, at least until noon." He stretched ostentatiously. "I don't know what to do with myself all morning. I suppose I'll have to go into the village to pass the time until our picnic."

"Picnic?"

Thomas gave her his devilish smile. "Oh, Kit, I forgot to tell you. Captain Montfort and the ladies have invited us over for a picnic today. We're going to explore the ruins of the old Norman fort up on the headland. Montfort thought you might enjoy it."

"I've seen the Norman ruins," Kitty said grumpily. "I don't care to go again."

Thomas looked innocent. "But, Kit, I thought you might want to go, and I accepted for you. Montfort told me that you and he had an appointment today to speak, so this will give you a chance for a long conversation."

"So he told you. I'm surprised, but I should have suspected the two of you would cook up something to keep me from finding out the truth. Are you going to be present?" Kitty understood Thomas's machinations.

"Of course not. Would I intrude on a private conversation?"

Kitty looked grimly at him. "You'd intrude on anything you had to if you thought it in your best interest."

Thomas strolled to the door and turned, blowing her a kiss. "Ah, Kit, you know me too well." He paused a second. "We're leaving around one. Marianne and Harriette are particularly looking forward to seeing you." With that, he went out the door before Kit could either say anything or throw a muffin at him.

Kit thought about pleading a headache, but knew Montfort would think she had cried off because she didn't want to face him, so she had to go. She became more and more nervous about the outing as the hour drew closer. Bidwell noted it and made several remarks about wedding nerves. Kitty had to bite her lip to keep from telling Bidwell how she really felt about nerves and weddings and Lord Richard in particular.

By the time the carriage to Sherbourne was drawn up in front, Kitty was not at all in charity with either Thomas or Richard, not even when Richard, looking particularly nice in a well-fitting buff coat and cream waistcoat, waited for her at the foot of the stairs. She was hard pressed not to snap at him when he told her how very fetching she looked in her jonquil muslin. Kit gritted her teeth together and determined that, once the carriage door had closed behind her, she was going to have a serious talk with both Richard and Thomas.

Thomas met her with a dazzling smile and opened the door of the carriage with a flourish. "Look who came over just to escort us to Sherbourne," he said, handing Kitty up into the seat. Kit tried to hide her grimace with a smile as she looked right into the simpering face of Harriette Marlowe.

"I told Ja . . . Captain Montfort that you would need company," she cooed. "After all, who wants to ride in a carriage with only two handsome gentlemen for company." She gave Richard and Thomas an arch look, which both seemed to be quite taken with.

"Very kind of you," Thomas murmured.

"Oh, not at all. Once Ja . . . Captain Montfort suggested it, I was more than glad to accompany Miss Walsingham."

Kitty looked up. "Captain Montfort suggested that you come over and accompany us?"

Harriette smiled. "Yes, he did. I remarked to dear Marianne how thoughtful her cousin was. Don't you think so?"

Kitty gave Thomas a look as Harriette waited for her reply. "Of course," she muttered through clenched teeth. "Captain Montfort's a complete paragon." Harriette might not know, but Kitty knew full well why Captain Montfort had sent someone along. It seemed they were all conspiring to keep Kitty from talking with anyone. Well, she thought to herself, they might be surprised. After all, they didn't realize how much she knew. Even Thomas didn't seem to believe that she knew the full extent of his participation in the smuggling. And as for Montfort—if he believed a picnic was going to get him out of his appointment with Kitty, he would be surprised. Kitty could see it all now: a picnic with everyone around, and Montfort carefully ignoring her while Thomas played the fool to distract her. They would be surprised this time.

Kitty settled back against the squabs with a determined look on her face. She would speak with Montfort, no matter what or who was around, and warn him away from Thomas. The captain could hang himself if he wished, but he was not going to drag her brother in with him.

Chapter Fifteen

When the carriage pulled up at Sherbourne, Kitty was amazed at the number of changes in the gardens and the outside since she had last been there. Montfort had been able to do a great deal in a short amount of time. And quite probably at great cost, Kitty thought to herself.

"Montfort has the place looking up, hasn't he?" Thomas said as they descended.

"The reward of ill-gotten gains," Kitty muttered under her breath. To her irritation, Thomas threw back his head and laughed heartily.

Montfort came down the front steps just then. "Glad to see you in such high humor, Thomas," he said, taking his hand.

"Just Kit again. I'll have to tell you what she said."

"Thomas." It was clearly a warning and for once, Thomas looked at her and took it. Even Montfort recognized her tone. "Perhaps later," he said to Thomas, after giving Kitty a hasty look. "Would you like to come in and see the changes I've made, or would you rather go right on to the ruins?"

"I'd rather go to the ruins," said Thomas at the very same time that Kitty said, "I'd love to see what you've done to the house."

Montfort looked from one to the other, then held out an arm to Kitty. "I yield to Miss Walsingham. It will only take a few moments."

As they mounted the stairs to the massive front door, a man came around the side of the house. Kitty recognized him at once as the man who had been talking to Montfort down at the *Erinys* the day before. Montfort seemed quite surprised at his presence. "Rachwood! I thought you had gone an hour since."

"Horse threw a shoe, and it was easier to walk back here than it was to try to get it fixed somewhere," Rachwood said, his pale eyes taking in the assembled company. "Tim down at the stables is fixing it right now. I'll be leaving in a few minutes."

Montfort drew out his pocket watch. "Can you make it to London before . . ." His words dangled off tantalizingly.

Rachwood just laughed. "James, you should know better than to ask that question of me. I've ridden all over France for you and haven't been late yet."

Montfort gave Kitty a look that was tinged with unease and excused himself politely. He took Rachwood by the arm and they went around the side of the house towards the stables. Kitty was overcome with curiosity and edged up to Thomas. "And just who was that man?" she whispered as Harriette led them into the house, just as if she were mistress there already.

"A friend of Montfort's," was Thomas's helpful reply.

"A likely story, Thomas," she whispered back, careful to stay at the back of the group—never mind that Thomas was dragging her past the door and down the hall. It was turning into something resembling a tug-of-war between them. Marianne turned and looked quizzically at them, and they both stopped and smiled sunnily at her. "Captain Montfort has done a superb job," Kitty said, not even noticing her surroundings. "Did you advise him?"

Marianne shook her head. "No, James did most of

171

this by himself. He even refused to accept Harriette's advice on the colors."

"Really?" That was the best thing Kitty had heard all day. She smiled steadfastly at Marianne until she went up to join Richard. Kitty was still hanging on to Thomas's arm. "Now, Thomas," she whispered again, "who is that man and what is he doing here?"

"I told you he's a friend of Montfort's, and how would I know what he's doing here?"

"I saw him down at the *Erinys* yesterday," she said.

"Perfectly logical place for him to be if he's visiting Montfort," Thomas replied, shoving her down the hall behind the others.

"And I suppose Montfort has dozens of friends who ride all over France for him?" Kitty asked acidly. "That's where all the contraband comes from, isn't it?"

"Don't be ridiculous," Thomas said.

"I'm not being ridiculous; I'm being perfectly logical. Now, I want to know who this man is and what he's doing here. And I want the truth, Thomas."

He pulled away from her. "If you want to know anything more, you'll have to ask Montfort yourself."

"I'll do just that," Kitty hissed at him as he left her and went up to join Harriette who was pointing out a rather ornate pair of drapes of French damask.

"French damask?" Kitty asked incredulously. "I wasn't aware that French damask could be bought in England. Wherever did Captain Montfort discover that?"

Thomas glared at her, Marianne's face turned a bright shade of pink, and Harriette merely looked at her. "There are ways, Miss Walsingham," Harriette said with a knowing smile. "I thought you already knew that."

"Touché," muttered Thomas, passing by her and following Harriette on into the next room.

Harriette had shown them through several rooms before Montfort joined them. Kitty had been amazed at the alterations the captain had made. Sherbourne had been turned into a house as elegant as any in London. Kitty had also been amazed at the profusion of French fabrics throughout the house. If there were ways, it seemed the captain knew all of them.

When Montfort joined them, he cut the tour short and suggested they leave at once for the ruins. "The grooms swear that we'll have rain late this afternoon, so I'd like to get started," he said by way of explanation. Kitty thought he was trying to get them away from the house. There had to be a connection with Rachwood's appearance.

There was no way to investigate, however, as they were hurried into the two waiting carriages. Montfort had even sent some servants ahead with the nuncheon, so there was no delay on that head. By now, Kitty was convinced that something was amiss. She tried to catch Thomas's eye, but he ignored her and very carefully made sure that he was seated in the other carriage. That put Montfort, Harriette, and Thomas in one carriage, with Marianne, Kitty, and Richard in the other, an arrangement not at all to Kitty's liking.

It was a good hour to the ruins, and the time was interminable. Richard and Marianne chatted on about gardens and drain tiles and the best time to prune roses while Kitty looked out the window and tried to fit Rachwood into the puzzle of the smuggling. The other two didn't seem to notice her preoccupation. She glanced at them once or twice, one time while they were avidly discussing the best type of soil and compost to use for herb gardens, another while Marianne was describing her excitement at seeing some gardens in Scotland. It was all well and good, Kitty thought. She wanted to sit and think about Montfort. It seemed all she had done for the past several days was think about him in one way or the other. Thomas was involved, but for how much? And now there was Rachwood, a thoroughly suspicious character if she had ever seen one. He, too, was involved in this imbroglio somewhere, she knew. She felt it in her bones.

When they reached the ruins, the servants already had nuncheon spread out on snowy cloths, waiting for them. Montfort, without a glance in Kitty's direction, managed to seat himself quite opposite her so there was no chance at all at conversation. As if she would mention so delicate a subject as smuggling in company! However, she did quite enjoy the fact that Montfort had positioned himself between Thomas and Marianne, leaving Harriette sitting between Thomas and Kitty. Harriette did not look at all amused, and had to spend the entire nuncheon blathering on to Kitty about goings-on in town and gossip about the *ton*. Evidently Montfort himself became so shamed by this obvious lack of manners that he eventually rose and seated himself between Thomas and Harriette. He was still careful not to get near Kitty.

Kitty surprised herself by being ravenous. There were several courses, among them lobster patties, duckling, some aspics, and, to Kitty's great joy, raspberry and strawberry tarts, prepared the French way with a custard inside. She was finishing her second tart when Harriette rose and went back to the carriage for her shawl. Montfort moved over toward Kitty, although not too close. "Did you enjoy your nuncheon?" he asked politely.

Kitty remembered not to lick her fingers and rummaged around for her serviette. "The tarts were delicious. I haven't had any like them since I was in France."

He smiled. "Ah, but I have managed to acquire a French chef. No one does pastry like the French. I do give credit where credit is due."

Kitty felt her eyebrows rise. "A French chef? Wasn't that difficult?"

"Not at all. Jacques was an émigré living in London.

He was glad for a position, and I was delighted to find a chef. Quite a mutually satisfactory arrangement."

Kitty looked at him. She couldn't decide if he was telling the truth or not. She never knew how to read Montfort. He returned her gaze and she blushed slightly. Montfort always seemed to be able to see right through her. She forced herself to meet his eyes and not look away. "I haven't forgotten our appointment," she said under her breath.

He smiled at her. "Nor have I, Miss Walsingham. I merely thought that, in light of yesterday's, ah, events, it would be wise to have some, ah, chaperones about."

At this, Kitty's face burned, and she bit her tongue to keep from embarrassing the entire company with a sharp retort. She glanced around to find Thomas looking curiously at her. She glared at him, then turned back to Montfort. "Chaperones or no, I intend to have my say, Captain Montfort."

"Certainly, Miss Walsingham." Kitty looked at him, sensing an undercurrent of laughter, but his expression was serious.

"Until later, Captain Montfort," she hissed.

He nodded at her as Harriette returned and sat down. "Your servant, Miss Walsingham," he said. Harriette looked at her through narrowed eyes as Kitty applied herself to the tarts once more.

After nuncheon, they wandered around the ruins. Harriette made quite a spectacle of herself, Kitty thought, hanging on to Montfort and declaring that she would fall every second. It was quite disgusting. Kitty herself had been to the ruins several times before and always enjoyed the trip. She scrambled over the rocks with familiarity until she reached the top of the pile of stones where she could see out across the Channel. She stood and looked across, feeling the sea breeze against her face. She had removed her bonnet and now lifted her face up to feel the sun and wind on it. It felt wonderful, like always.

"Longing for France?" It was a murmur behind her, and she didn't even have to turn around to know who it was. Every time he spoke in a low tone to her, there was a husky quality in his voice. She would recognize it anywhere.

"And if I were?"

"Then I should take you there, Miss Walsingham," Montfort said, climbing up to stand beside her and looking across the water.

"I'm sure you know the way," she snapped. "All those French silks in Sherbourne had to come from somewhere."

"And they did," he answered, looking down at her with laughter in his eyes. He looked at her for a long moment, a gaze Kitty returned. The sun was glinting on his hair again, and there were golden lights in his amber eyes. Remembering yesterday, she felt herself go weak again, and a strange sensation begin in her knees and travel upward. Forgetting the others, all she could think of was that she wished he would kiss her again. She was intensely aware of him, and she thought, he of her. His arm brushed against hers, and she longed to feel it around her. Montfort, too, had a strange, faraway look on his face as he gazed at her. He licked his lips slowly, as though trying to decide something. Then his expression altered to the slightly arrogant look that Kitty was beginning to learn hid his emotions. "I don't think this is the place for our talk, Miss Walsingham. Perhaps we should join the others," he said huskily.

Without a word, Kitty turned and made her way down the rocks, concentrating her gaze on her feet so she wouldn't stumble, and ignoring Montfort's proffered hand. If she touched him, she knew, she would throw herself on him, right there in front of everyone.

Harriette watched Kitty and Montfort come down the stones, her face a hard mask of cheerfulness. Once they were down, she wasted no time, walking directly up to Kitty and stepping between Kitty and Montfort. "Dear Catherine," she chirped, "I understand from Thomas that you are quite familiar with these ruins. Thomas tells me you've explored up here since you were a small child, so perhaps you might help me."

"Help you?" Kitty was blank. She still hadn't recovered from the sensations caused by Montfort's nearness.

"Yes, dear." Harriette smiled at her, and drew her away from Montfort. "There is a strange carving on a stone over here, and I do wish you would explain it to me." Harriette tucked her arm in Kitty's and led her to the edge of the ruin.

Kitty looked around, frowning. "There are no remains this far out, Harriette. I'm sure you must be mistaken." By this time, they were well away from the others.

"Unfortunately, I am seldom mistaken in matters such as this," Harriette said, releasing her arm and turning to face her. "What I wish to know has nothing to do with a pile of old rocks." She spoke in a low voice.

"What is it you wish to know?" Kitty asked, her mind still on Montfort.

"I wish to know why you keep casting sheep's eyes at Captain Montfort, Miss Walsingham," Harriette snapped. "As I said, I am seldom mistaken in matters such at this, and I can see you are clearly infatuated with the captain." Harriette's face was twisted in anger, and her voice shook. "I also wish to tell you, dear Miss Walsingham, that your schemes will do you no good. I assure you that the captain is quite spoken for."

"What!" Kitty couldn't believe her ears. "I can tell you that nothing could be farther from my mind."

"Really?" Harriette lifted an eyebrow. "I've seen these

symptoms before, Miss Walsingham. I believe the last time I saw you this way, you were thoroughly infatuated with that simpering calfling in London."

Kitty's face flamed red, but Harriette continued, her face still contorted with rage. "And I'm quite sure you remember that you didn't have a chance once I set my mind to take him away from you. I assure you, *dear* Catherine, that episode was nothing compared to this. I mean to wed the captain, and I will brook no interference."

"Have you informed the captain of your plans?" Kitty snapped back at her. "Or are you planning to tell him later?"

"My plans are no concern of yours," Harriette said, refusing to meet her eyes. "However," she looked up at Kitty as she spoke, "I wonder how Lord Richard would feel about his future bride throwing herself on the captain in such a manner."

"I have never thrown myself on the captain or anyone else," Kitty said. She was beginning to feel the beginnings of, not just anger, but pure rage. The nerve of the woman!

"Be that as it may, Miss Walsingham, I'm warning you. Stay away from Captain Montfort."

"That's difficult to do when he's in Thomas's pocket night and day. And, I assure *you*, Miss Marlowe, that I think of Captain Montfort in no other way than I do my own brother. In fact, . . ." Kitty paused, then stopped. She really didn't want to analyze her feelings for Montfort.

"In fact, what, Miss Walsingham?"

"In fact, there have been times when I didn't care at all for the captain, either as a friend of mine or as a friend for Thomas." Kitty looked at her coolly. "To be truthful, Miss Marlowe, I usually considered the captain in the same way I considered you. I wish you well of him. The two of you should be perfectly matched." With that, Kitty turned and walked back toward the others sitting at the ruins. She fought down her anger, and by the time she had reached them, she was able to speak in a level voice.

"What kind of Banbury tale have you been telling Harriette?" Thomas asked her with a grin. "I told James that you were probably inventing the ghost of a marauding Norman to go with the ruins."

"Hardly," Kitty said, taking a seat beside Thomas on a rock, carefully away from Montfort. "Actually, what I was telling her was quite the truth."

Thomas grinned again as Harriette came walking up to them and sat down near Montfort. Harriette's face was a careful mask, and she tried to hide the anger in her eyes, but failed. Thomas turned to Montfort. "Thought Kit was inventing some smugglers to hide here in the rocks. Do you suppose so? Pirates and all that sort of thing?"

"I'm sure Kitty would do nothing of the sort," Montfort answered with a smile. Kitty caught nothing except his use of her name. It was the first time he had used it, and his voice seemed to slide over the sounds. She glanced at him, but was unable to return his smile.

"I'm getting quite fatigued," Harriette said, with an arch look up at Montfort. "Could we be getting back now? I need to rest before supper."

"A good suggestion," Montfort said. "I've invited Thomas, Kitty, and Richard over for supper and an evening of cards. Thomas has accepted for everyone."

"How very exciting," Harriette said, her voice very flat.

Marianne looked up momentarily. She and Richard were discussing apple orchards, most especially about locating them on the north side so the buds wouldn't bloom too early and get killed by frost. "I'm so glad

179

you're going to be with us, Kitty. Thomas has even promised that you might sing for us."

Kitty glared at Thomas. He saw her look and got away before she could say anything. With much bustling, they got in the carriages in the same way they had ridden up, and returned. At Sherbourne, Kitty, Richard, and Thomas were all in one carriage for the trip home, with Thomas promising to have everyone back for supper. Kitty didn't dare speak, for fear of causing bodily harm to her father's only heir. "Cheer up, Kit," Thomas said with a grin at her. "Tonight you can really shine. By the by, just what did you say to Harriette to get her up into the boughs so? I've wondered all the way home."

"I told her I didn't care for her," Kitty said shortly. "Actually, Thomas, after accepting an invitation from Montfort without consulting me, I don't particularly care for you right now either."

"Nothing new," Thomas said, then turned his attention to Richard. "Did you and Miss Montfort have an enjoyable cose?"

Richard beamed. "Capital! Do you know that she'd helped her father around his estate and knows all about farming? I just can't believe a mere woman would know those things!"

"Lord knows I wouldn't," Thomas said. "What do you know about farming, Kit?"

Richard's head snapped up at the mention of Kitty's name. "Oh, I don't expect Kit to know about farming. She'll be far too busy with the household and nursery to worry about the estate. I'll do that."

The carriage arrived at Bellevoir, much to Kitty's relief. Without a word, she scrambled out and angrily stomped into the house, going so rapidly past Duff that he barely had time to move away.

She could hear Thomas laughing behind her.

Chapter Sixteen

Kit toyed with the idea of coming down with a convenient headache to keep from going to Montfort's, but decided that was the coward's way out. Still, it was one of those times when she wished she could be a craven coward. Instead, she resignedly told Bidwell to order her a bath and lay out some suitable clothes. Bidwell was overjoyed, and spent the afternoon fussing about in Kitty's wardrobe. By the time Bidwell was finished with her toilette, Kitty was quite turned out in her newest gown of pale nile with an underskirt of deeper green. Bidwell had put curls around her face and intertwined ribands in the curls. Even Kitty hated to admit it, but she had to agree with Bidwell's comment that she looked fetching.

When she went downstairs, she was met by Thomas. "By Jove, Kit, you're going to put the rest of the assembly in the shade," he said, standing back to look at her.

"The assembly? Whatever are you talking about, Thomas? There will only be the six of us."

Thomas looked slightly discomfited. "That's why I wanted to meet you here and explain," he began.

Kit stared at him. "Explain? Explain what, Thomas. If you've cozened me again, I warn you . . ."

"I wouldn't do that, Kit, you know me better," he said, giving her a reproachful look she ignored. "There is one thing, though."

"And that is . . . ," she prompted.

"Well, Montfort invited us all over some time ago, and I was supposed to tell you about it. I know he said today that it was an evening of supper and cards, but that ain't exactly it." He stopped again, but Kitty remained silent, forcing him to continue. "He asked me if you were coming, and I said yes."

Kitty's eyes narrowed as she looked at him. "Exactly what are you saying, Thomas?"

"It's a party, Kit. There will be about twenty there, I think. I don't exactly know the reason for it, but from what hints Harriette has dropped, I'm afraid it's a party to announce her and Montfort's engagement to the country." He took her hand. "I know how you feel about Harriette, and if you want to cry off now, I'll be sure to make your excuses."

Kitty stiffened. "Nonsense. What Captain Montfort and Harriette Marlowe do or don't do is of no concern of mine. I do wish you had told me, though. I might have worn something else."

"Believe me, you look capital." There was obvious relief in Thomas's voice. "Are you sure an announcement won't bother you?"

"Quite sure." Kitty made her voice firm, but she was unable to meet Thomas's eyes. The thought of Montfort and Harriette was almost too much to bear, but it was something she was going to have to face. It was evidently true: Harriette always got what she wanted.

"I know," Thomas said. "We could also announce that you and Richard are engaged!" He grinned at her. "Wouldn't that set all the local tabbies on their ears!" He paused and looked at Kitty. "Not to mention taking the wind right out of Harriette's sails."

"No!" The word was louder than Kitty had intended. "I mean it, Thomas, no. I'm not ready to announce anything."

He looked at her sharply. "Richard thinks you are."

"I'm not sure, Thomas. I don't think I love Richard enough to marry him." She looked back at him, but her expression was troubled.

"Oh, Lord," Thomas groaned. "That old tale again. Listen to me, Kit," he began, but was interrupted by Maman and Papa coming down the stairs.

"I see you are both ready, and you look lovely, ma petite," Maman said.

Kitty took in her mother's evening dress of violet trimmed with black. "You are going with us, Maman?" she asked, surprised.

"Of course, dear. Captain Montfort quite charmed us into visiting him. Quite a fine young man."

If you only knew, Kitty thought to herself as she followed them out to the carriage. It didn't occur to her until Thomas handed her up into the seat to ask about Richard. "Shouldn't we wait for Richard? Where will he sit?"

Thomas gave her a telling glance. "Richard rode over about a half hour ago. He said there wouldn't be room in the carriage, and since it was more convenient for him to ride, he'd do that."

"A fine young man," Maman echoed again. Papa caught Kitty's eye and smiled at her as though he knew what was going through her mind. Kitty had trouble identifying the emotion but finally realized it was relief. It was yet another reason she must talk with Richard, and soon. There was no point in carrying on this charade.

Sherbourne was lit with candles, and the windows sparkled as they drove up. It seemed to Kitty that the entire county was there. Harriette must have planned the entire evening.

"Chin up," Thomas muttered to her as they entered.

"Don't worry about me," she whispered back, going in the door and almost running right into Montfort.

He stepped back and took in her gown. "That color becomes you, Miss Walsingham," he said, reaching for her hand, then thinking the better of it and moving away. He smiled at her briefly and then went on to greet Thomas, Papa, and Maman. Kitty waited for a polite moment, then allowed Thomas to escort her into the drawing room. Harriette was there, holding court over the local gentry, and they seemed duly impressed. Harriette was looking particularly striking in rose pink, a simple gown that proclaimed its richness in the fabric. Even Thomas noticed. "Fifty guineas," he said, "don't you think."

"At least," Kitty answered, giving the gown a critical look. "I'd say it's from Madame Bertolle, and it looks like French silk."

Thomas chuckled. "I think I'm going to make a regular member of the *ton* out of you yet. Give me another six months."

"I don't intend to give you anything," Kitty retorted. "I don't see how Montfort and Richard manage to abide being around you."

"Speaking of Richard," Thomas said, giving Kitty a nudge toward the garden windows.

Kitty looked and saw Richard, deep in conversation with Marianne. They seemed completely oblivious to everyone else in the room. "Kit," Thomas said to her in a serious tone, "you're going to have to make up your mind and tell Richard something. *He* thinks he's engaged to you, and this looks amazingly like a complication."

Kitty looked at Richard and Marianne. "They're probably talking about drainage tiles again. It would be a good match, wouldn't it?"

"I'm not going to say," Thomas said. "Meanwhile, I hate to set you adrift, but I see Mrs. Brathwaite bearing down on us, and she has that ugly daughter of hers in tow. What's the chit's name—Ameline, Adelaide?"

Kitty laughed. "Her name is Barbara, and you could do worse. She'd besotted with you, you know."

"Oh, Lord, no! Kit, I can't imagine anything worse at

the moment. I'll see you later." With that, he melted into the crowd and began a conversation with one of the Taylor boys, leaving Kitty to cope with Mrs. Brathwaite and Barbara.

"Lovely party," said Mrs. Brathwaite, giving Thomas a forlorn look, now that her quarry had fled. "Lovely," echoed Barbara. "Lovely," said Kitty, edging away. Mrs. Brathwaite wasn't interested in her, and began making her way, Barbara in tow, toward the Taylor boys and Thomas.

Kitty stood back near the garden window and surveyed the group. There were, as Thomas had said, about twenty to twenty-five there, most of them local gentry. Harriette was doing it up quite brown, Kitty thought. She had no more time for reflection as supper was announced then, and Thomas fled from Mrs. Brathwaite and Barbara to Kitty's side. "Tell me you need an escort into supper," he gasped, looking nervously at Barbara.

"I should let you flounder like a fish on the hook," she said, "but I suppose I should have pity on you. Do you suppose Richard feels obligated to escort me in?"

"Well, he should," Thomas said, taking her arm just before Mrs. Brathwaite reached them, "but I do believe, Kit, that he's otherwise occupied." He nodded in the direction of Richard, who was going into the dining room with Marianne on his arm.

"Have I been jilted, Thomas?" Kit asked, trying to keep her voice light. Somehow, Richard had always been in the back of her mind, someone she could always rely on if she needed to.

"I think you'd better get out of that entanglement while you still can with some dignity. Besides, Richard will think about you soon, and he'll feel a duty to live up to what he considers his obligation. Richard's that way."

"I know—one of Maman's fine young men."

Thomas laughed and sat her down at the table. They

were seated directly across from Richard and Marianne. Richard looked up and saw Kitty there for the first time. His face turned red, and he stuttered as he spoke to her. "Good to see you, Kitty. You're looking very fine tonight. I didn't realize you were here or I would have . . ." His voice trailed off as he gazed from her to Marianne. "I'm sorry." He looked thoroughly miserable.

Kitty smiled at him. "Quite all right, Richard. Thomas was good enough to escort me. I'm delighted you thought to escort Marianne in." Kitty glanced at Marianne, and she looked as miserable as Richard. Clearly, Kitty thought to herself as she looked around the rest of the table, she was going to have to talk to Richard this very night. Marianne seemed quite taken with him, and Kitty thought it wonderful that it might be Marianne and not herself who would be sitting beside Richard for eternity discussing drainage tiles. Surprisingly, the thought brought no feeling of regret.

Kitty forced herself back to the assembly at hand. Harriette was sitting at the end of the table opposite Montfort, the place Marianne as his hostess should have occupied. Clearly, Harriette already thought herself mistress of Sherbourne.

The supper was elegant, and Montfort's French chef outdid himself. Each course was greeted with amazement and compliments, but Kitty found herself unable to eat very much. She spent most of the meal pushing food around on her plates, hoping no one would notice. Finally, it was time for the women to withdraw to the saloon, and she was relieved. The evening already seemed interminable.

Once in the saloon, Harriette again took charge of the group, leading the conversation and placing herself in what should have been Marianne's place. "Forward girl," a voice murmured beside Kitty. She looked around to find Mrs. Brathwaite beside her. "I suppose that's how they do things in the *ton,* but, I assure you, Miss Walsingham, that I and my Barbara would never stoop to such antics! Why, that woman's just taken over, and her and the captain ain't even properly engaged." Mrs. Brathwaite fanned herself vigorously. "A scandal, that's what it is." She sniffed audibly. Another tabby on the other side of Mrs. Brathwaite took up the conversation, much to Kitty's relief. She didn't want to comment on Harriette's behavior, because she knew she would be quoted far and wide.

The gentlemen, much to everyone's surprise, joined them in just a very few minutes. Marianne and Harriette joined to entertain the group on the pianoforte, and a small local band played as well. There was quite a crowd in the saloon, as large as the room was. Stifled, Kitty moved over against the French door to try to get some fresh air. After standing there by herself like a wallflower for a few minutes, she decided to slip out into the garden. After all, she wouldn't be at all missed, she decided; everyone seemed to be quite occupied.

The garden was fragrant, but even this far from the beach she could scent the tang of the sea. The evening was cool enough to be just right to walk on the grounds. She was standing near the corner of the house, enjoying the heady scent of the phlox planted in the garden borders, when she heard a soft footfall behind her. She turned, halfway expecting Thomas. Her smile and the bantering words she was going to say stopped as the shadowy shape stepped into the moonlight, and she recognized him. It was Montfort. Without thinking, she took a step back, almost against the wall.

"Did I startle you?" he asked softly. "If I did, I'm sorry."

"No." Kitty was instantly aware of him. It was as if she knew everything about the shape of him, and was aware of him all over. "I must get back," she said, trying to slip by him to someplace where she could breathe again.

"Please." He reached out and held her by the arm. He wasn't holding tightly, but a tingle ran down Kitty's arm. Then he pulled her closer. "I wanted to talk to you."

"I thought we agreed we had nothing to say unless chaperones were about." Kitty wanted to step back again, but he faced her, his eyes enormous and dark in the moonlight. His voice was husky as he spoke to her.

"I thought so, too, but this afternoon as we stood and looked out to sea together, I realized that we have very many things to say to each other, most of them quite private."

Kitty was having trouble breathing; all she could sense was the nearness of him, the sweet, spicy smell of the phlox mixed with the smell of his soap and body. "No," she whispered, but she couldn't say more because his lips were on hers. He kissed her softly at first, toying gently with her lower lip. Then he held her closer as he whispered in her ear, "Catherine, sweet Catherine." The words slid off his tongue like honey as he kissed a trail across her cheek back to her mouth. Then he kissed her again, completely this time, and held her against him. She could feel the length of his body against hers, and she pressed herself against him, wanting him as much as he wanted her. She felt a slight pressure against her ribs as he put his hand there and moved her back against the wall, its slight roughness and chill against her back a contrast to his warmth against the front of her body. He kissed her softly along her collarbone and in the hollow of her throat as his fingertips moved up her arm and across the bareness exposed by the décolletage of her dress. Each touch, light as it was, was like a slow burn against her skin.

"Catherine," he whispered again, his fingertips tracing the outline of her face in the shadow. She couldn't have stopped him if she had wanted to — and she didn't want to.

Suddenly he stiffened and drew her back into the shadow against the wall. "Ssshh," he murmured in her ear, standing in front of her to shield her pale dress from view. In just a moment, Kitty heard what he had heard—an impatient footfall along the garden path. She moved even closer to the wall as she recognized Richard walking by.

After a moment, Montfort moved out. "I think he's gone around the corner, but he'll be back in a moment. I suppose he's looking for you?"

"I don't know. It doesn't signify."

He gave her the ghost of a smile. "Perhaps for you, but keep in mind that I'm the one Richard will be forced to call out if we're discovered." He peered at her face. "Perhaps you'd better wait a few moments before going back into the light."

Kitty reached up and touched her bruised lips. Her whole face felt swollen and bruised. "Do I look that bad?"

He smiled again. "No. I think you look even more beautiful than usual, but then, I'm quite prejudiced." He took her hand. "There's a bench over here where you can sit for a moment, then we'll go back in."

Kitty sat down and Montfort stood beside her. Again she was aware of him, still feeling the pressure of his lips on her skin. The thought made her lips and skin tingle. "Perhaps we should go in separately," she suggested. "I can wait here until Richard returns."

"I suppose it would be better. Are you sure you'll be all right? I don't want you to get a chill."

Kitty laughed aloud. "Keep in mind that I'm no London miss, Captain Montfort. Weather like this won't give me a chill."

There was a voice behind them. "A chill, Miss Walsingham," said Harriette in a sneering voice. "I thought that trick had gone out before the Revolution." She stopped and gazed at Montfort. "However, you seem to be able to employ it to great advantage."

Montfort drew himself up. "You're quite mistaken, Harriette. Miss Walsingham came out to the garden for a few moments, and I merely came out to see if she was all right. Lord Richard will be back in a few moments." He stared at Harriette coldly. "You may wish to apologize to Miss Walsingham."

"I don't apologize for telling the truth," Harriette snapped. "The only thing I may do, James, is tell you what a cake you're making of yourself following Miss Walsingham around. You've embarrassed me in front of the whole assembly."

"I hardly think so," Montfort said with ice in his voice. "I see no reason for this scene, and think you might need to go to your chamber to calm yourself. You're seeing illusions, Harriette."

"Illusions! Humbug! I'll tell you exactly what I'm seeing. I'm seeing some country chit trying . . ."

"That's quite enough," Montfort snapped, interrupting her. "I don't want to hear any more. Miss Walsingham is a guest here at Sherbourne as, may I remind you, are you. I will *not* have my guests insulted."

Harriette stood up taller. "I see," she said slowly. "When you find out just what kind of person your dear Miss Walsingham is, James, don't come running to me."

"I hadn't planned on it, Harriette."

They stood there, looking daggers at each other when Richard came around the corner.

"I say, Montfort, there you are. Been looking all over for you." He stopped and looked down at Kitty. "You all right, Kit? You're looking a little peaked." Then without waiting for a reply, he turned his attention to Montfort. "Ran into a couple of fellows at the back of the house who said they had to see you on some urgent business of some kind or the other. I've been looking for you ever since."

"Who?" Montfort asked, but Richard was already turning back to the corner of the house. "This way," Richard said in a very loud voice. "The captain's here."

Kitty heard Montfort's quick intake of breath as Rachwood and another man walked around the corner. "Thank God you're home, Montfort," said Rachwood. He was dusty and travel-stained, his boots covered with mud. The man with him looked even worse.

"I thought you were on your way to London," Montfort said. Rachwood glanced at Richard, Harriette, and Kitty. "I was, but I ran into Waters here on the way. He's got important news, and a message from . . ."

Montfort threw up a hand to stop Rachwood from speaking. "Lord Richard, will you see that Miss Marlowe and Miss Walsingham are returned to the saloon? I'm afraid I won't be able to see them in."

Richard, usually fairly obtuse, almost jumped. "Of course," he said, almost jerking Kitty up off the bench. He handled Harriette almost as roughly, taking her arm and almost throwing her off balance. "I'm quite able to see myself in," she said icily, moving away and walking in front of them.

Kitty allowed Richard to lead her in, but she took one last backwards glance at Montfort. He spoke briefly to the two men, took a paper from Waters, then the three of them broke into a run. The last Kitty saw of him was a glance in her direction as he rounded the corner of the house.

She went indoors and looked for Thomas. He was standing, being entertained by Mrs. Braithwaite and her Barbara, and had an unbelievably pained expression on his face. Ignoring propriety, Kitty walked up and took his arm. "Thomas, I have to see you immediately." She glanced at Mrs. Braithwaite's shocked face and murmured, "Pardon us" as she moved Thomas over to a deserted corner.

"Thanks, Kit," Thomas said. "It isn't often I need rescuing, but that was one time. I owe you a favor."

"You can repay it now," Kitty said, quickly telling him about Rachwood and Waters coming and of Montfort's reaction. "I think something is wrong, Thomas," she said. "Let's go see what's happening."

"Are you *sure* it was Rachwood and Waters?" Thomas demanded.

"Of course I'm sure. Thomas, I know you're involved in this smuggling, but you have to save James. If scmeone s coming to catch him, you need to warn him."

Thomas lifted an eyebrow. "James? Is that how the land lays, Kit? I thought you didn't like him and wanted him caught."

Kitty felt her face flame. "Please, Thomas." She caught her underlip with her teeth. "You're as involved as he is. You owe it to him to help. The very least you can do is warn him. He could get on the *Erinys* and be gone in a very few minutes."

Thomas looked at her. "All right, Kit. I'll go see what's happening, but I'm going alone. Is that clear? I don't want you following along to stumble right into the middle of anything."

"Just go, Thomas. Please."

He left her and slipped out the garden door. Harriette saw him leave and gave Kitty a menacing look. Kitty saw that Harriette was heading her way, so she made her way to her father, asking if they could leave, and pleading a headache.

Papa looked at her in surprise, but seeing the pain and misery in her expression, gave way immediately. Maman wouldn't hear of staying either, saying she would inform Thomas. Kitty hastily told them that she had already told Thomas, and he had suggested they go ahead, and he would return with Richard.

By the time they arrived at Bellevoir, Kitty truly had a crashing headache.

Chapter Seventeen

Bidwell helped Kitty undress and gave her a tisane for her headache, then put her to bed with a cloth soaked in lavender water on her head. Kitty dozed for a little while, but awoke when the candle guttered. For a moment she lay there, wondering vaguely about her feeling of unease, until she remembered the scene with Montfort at Sherbourne. Had Thomas discovered anything, she wondered, sitting up in the bed and lighting another candle. She tossed a robe over her nightrail and went to Thomas's room, knocking softly. There was no answer. "Thomas," she whispered, knocking again. When there was still no answer, she opened the door. Thomas was not there, and his bed had not been slept in.

Kitty heard the hall clock chime two as she went back to her room. She blew out her candle and looked out the window. The night was clear, and she could see the moon shining on the water of the Channel. She almost turned away from the window, but then she saw it out of the corner of her eye—just a glimmer, a flash of light, lasting only for a moment. It was so short that she wondered if she saw it at all, but then, in a minute, it was followed by another flash. This time she recognized it. This time it was unmistakably a flare from a quickly shuttered lantern.

Moving quickly, Kitty drew out her dark gown and her pattens and put them on, fumbling in the dark as she dressed. She dared not light her candle—whoever was down at the beach might see that she was awake and leave. Finally she was dressed, except for a tangle of hair. Groping blindly in the dark, she found a riband on her dressing table that she quickly used to bind back her hair. She grabbed her dark cloak and slipped out the door, carrying her pattens so she wouldn't make any noise as she went down the hall to the stairs. As she passed by Richard's door, she heard the sound of gentle snoring, so he was evidently not with Thomas. She wondered briefly why he hadn't awakened the household when he discovered Thomas missing. Perhaps he hadn't worried because he was accustomed to Thomas leading his own life in London and keeping his own hours.

At the back door, Kitty put on her pattens and started down the path to the beach, keeping to one side to take shelter in the bracken if she had to. It seemed the way to the beach in the dark had become familiar to her since Montfort moved next door. How, she wondered to herself, just how could he be a smuggler? She hadn't been able to answer that question at all. The more she knew of him, the more convinced she was that he couldn't be involved. But then, she kept reminding herself, there was the evidence of her own eyes.

At the top of the cliff, Kitty paused and hid, peering around a bush until she could look down at the *Erinys*. She thought she saw someone, only a dark shape on the deck, but she couldn't be certain. She paused, waiting for what seemed like an eternity, but didn't see any movement at all. Still, she was sure there must be someone there. Someone had to answer that lantern flash.

Carefully, avoiding loose rocks, she made her way down to the foot of the cliff and hid in the same place she had hidden before. There still seemed to be no movement; there was only the wind rippling the water and sighing through the sea grasses. Kitty moved down and made her way across the beach, keeping as close to the sand as possible. Finally she reached the wooden dock and stopped. Her pattens would make too much noise on the planks, so she sat beside the large, weathered posts that anchored the dock and took them off, leaving them in the sand. Barefooted, she went down the dock and onto the short gangplank. Once aboard, she was sure she heard voices and she dropped to the deck, huddling as close to the rail as she could.

After a few moments of listening in the silence of the night, she decided she had been letting her imagination play tricks on her, and she moved across the deck. She didn't want to take any chances on being seen, so she stayed on her hands and knees, scuttling across the deck like a crab. She was almost to the cabin door when, without any warning, someone grabbed her from behind and clapped a hand roughly over her mouth. She tried to bite, but it was no use. Whoever was holding her was much stronger and had the advantage of being on top of her. Still she tried to fight, but he wrestled her to the deck, flattening her out on the deck and covering her with his body. Finally, she lay still, her cloak almost off and the riband holding her hair gone, leaving her hair spread in a tumble across her shoulders and the deck.

The man above her whispered harshly, "You little fool!"

She recognized Montfort's voice, and made a gurgling sound into the hand that was still on her mouth. "What in the name of God are you doing here at this time of night? Don't you know it's dangerous?" His body lay along the length of hers, pressing her into the deck. Kitty was conscious of a strange feeling, as the warmth of him came through her tumbled cloak. She mumbled into his palm, and he released his hand momentarily.

"Of course I know . . . ," Kitty began, but he clapped his hand over her mouth again.

"Ssshhh," he whispered in her ear, his breath hot against her skin. "There are others out there. Promise me you'll be quiet and follow me." He waited, but Kitty made no sign. "Promise me, Kitty, or I swear I'll tie and gag you right here. You know I will."

Kitty nodded her head, and he moved his hand slightly. "All right, I promise," she croaked.

He moved his hand away, and she drew a deep breath. Then he rolled easily off of her, her body suddenly light after the pressure of his weight on her. For a second, she was tempted to jump up and run, but as if he could read her mind, he reached out. "Stay down and crawl after me," he whispered. "If you don't, you're going to ruin everything." He paused, his face grim in the moonlight. "That is, if you haven't already."

"Just what do you . . ."

"Quiet, dammit." It was almost a growl and Kitty, recognizing a command when she heard one, stayed quiet. Montfort crawled along the deck, staying close to the cabin wall until he reached the door. Kitty crawled right along behind him. At the door, he reached up and pushed it open a little, only enough to allow him and Kitty to crawl through. He didn't relax until she was through the door, and he had pushed it closed behind them. He stayed on the floor, leaning back against the cabin wall, and motioned for her to do the same. She leaned back against the wall near him. It was too dark in the cabin for Kitty to see very much. There was moonlight coming in the cabin window, but it didn't shine on Montfort.

"Now, Miss, perhaps you'll tell me what you're doing here at this time of night." His voice was cold.

"I couldn't sleep," Kitty said, and it sounded lame even to her. "I saw some flashes of light down here and thought I'd come down to see . . ." Her words trailed off.

"Catching smugglers again?" He was pure sarcasm.

"You should know," she retorted. "If you really are interested, I was worried about Thomas. It would kill Maman and Papa if Thomas was caught smuggling. Perhaps you don't mind breaking the law, but Thomas isn't that sort of person."

She could hear Montfort exhale deeply. "Miss Walsingham, whatever are you talking about?"

"I'm talking about you corrupting Thomas," she said, then lowered her voice at his whispered "Ssshhh." "I'm talking about you taking a young man who admires you and turning him into a criminal."

"Oh, God," Montfort said. "Kitty—Miss Walsingham, I promise you that I'll explain everything later. I promise you that there is an explanation—a very reasonable one. All I ask is that you go home now, before you completely wreck everything."

"Are you afraid of what I'll discover, Captain?"

He turned and shook her roughly. "No, Kitty, I'm not. If you knew me at all, you'd know that such ideas about me are contrary to everything I've ever done or stood for." He was right next to her, his face close to hers. "I'd hoped you'd come to know me better than that." He put his fingers on her face. "I'd hoped . . ."

"I'd hoped, too," Kitty answered, not needing for him to complete his sentence. "I'd hoped for so much." She thought he was going to kiss her again, and wanted nothing more in the world. She leaned into him, wanting him to touch her, wanting him to do other things to her.

His fingertips made a trail along her cheekbone. "Catherine," he whispered. "I wish . . ."

Suddenly it was as if the world outside exploded into a blaze. There was shouting and the sound of gunfire. Montfort jumped to his feet and pushed Kitty to the floor. "Whatever you do, don't leave this cabin," he said roughly. "I promise everything will be all right." With that, he was out the door, running across the deck and leaping the railing onto the dock. Kitty dared to stand enough to peer out the cabin window. She could hardly stand to watch Montfort running down to the beach, afraid that at any minute he would be caught either by a constable or by the gunfire.

He reached the beach, and she lost sight of him as he melted into the darkness at the edge of the cliff. Kitty looked vainly into the darkness, but could see nothing. There was a volley of gunfire from one side of the beach, and then she could hear Montfort shouting orders to someone, telling them to hold their fire. She was sick at heart. "Oh, James," she mumbled to herself. "God help you." It didn't matter at all if he were a criminal or if he weren't, She only knew she needed for him to be safe.

She stayed in the cabin, terrified, unable to make any sense of the shadowy forms running across the beach, unable to see what was happening. She wanted to go out and try to find Thomas, but knew it was impossible. If he was with Montfort, he was all right. James would take care of him, he had promised.

As suddenly as it had begun, the noise and gunfire was over. The stillness descended quickly, taking Kitty unaware. She looked again out the window, and saw several men heading toward the *Erinys*. There were several who were obviously prisoners of the others, but she couldn't see well enough to make out the faces. She looked around for a weapon to use if it should be James and Thomas who were the prisoners. She was rummaging in James's desk drawer when someone slipped in the cabin door. Quickly she dropped behind the desk.

"Kitty?" It was a hoarse whisper.

"Thomas!" Kitty said, throwing herself at him. "You're all right! James? Is James all right?"

"For God's sake, Kitty, be quiet."

Kitty was worried that he hadn't answered her.

"Thomas, I have to know—is James all right?"

"Yes." Thomas held her and twisted to look out the cabin window. "He told me you were in here. What kind of fool idea did you have, Kit?"

"It wasn't . . ."

Thomas interrupted her. "James sent me in to see if I could get you off the *Erinys* before everyone gets on board." He took another quick look out the cabin window. "Oh, God, here they come. It's too late. Kitty, your reputation is a shambles." Desperately he looked around and saw the outlines of a sea chest in the moonlight. "Here," he said, shoving her toward the chest. "Get in here and keep your mouth shut. It's our only chance."

In just a moment they had emptied the chest and tossed the contents, mainly cloaks and clothing for rainy weather, behind the chest. As they heard the voices nearing the cabin door, Thomas shoved Kitty unceremoniously in and started to lower the lid.

"You wouldn't leave me here to suffocate, would you, Thomas?"

He stared at her. "Don't be an ass, Kit. Here, get down, and whatever you do, don't sneeze. I'll let you out as soon as it's safe." Thomas slammed the lid down and left Kitty in the dark. From the noise, she thought he sat on it, evidently taking no chances. Thomas had never trusted her to do what she said she would do.

She heard the sound of the cabin door opened roughly and the sounds of the men filing in. Then she heard Montfort ordering the door shut. "Now Mr. Braithwaite," she heard him say, "I don't think a confession is necessary in view of the fact that we caught you with the information, but it might go easier if you named some other names. Would you like to write out your confession here, or had you rather be taken to London to tell it personally to the Home Office?"

Kitty strained her ears, but could hear no reply. She

wondered what Mr. Braithwaite was doing there. Whatever was James talking about? The air in the chest was musty, and she felt herself ready to sneeze. With the greatest effort, she suppressed it. She tried to lift the lid a fraction so she could see out and get some fresh air, but hard as she pushed, she couldn't budge it at all. Evidently Thomas was still sitting on it.

She could hear murmuring, but couldn't make out the words. Then someone came over and sat on the chest with Thomas. "Lord, I never thought the captain could pull it off, did you?" As best as Kitty could tell, it was Rachwood speaking. He continued. "How he managed to crack them is a mystery, but then the captain could always do the impossible."

Thomas shifted uneasily. "He certainly can. Do you think they'll stay here long, or will they leave and take these vermin to gaol? I thought they'd be right on their way to Portsmouth."

Rachwood laughed. "I imagine the captain will squeeze every last drop of information out of them before he lets someone else have a crack at them. He's a master of that." Rachwood shifted on the top of the chest. "Funny what men will do for money, isn't it? Who would have thought it of someone who appeared to be a fine, upstanding citizen like Braithwaite here?"

Thomas was not in the mood for philosophical discussions. "Do you think you could suggest taking everybody to Portsmouth?"

Rachwood's voice was incredulous. "What? And miss seeing the captain work them over? I guarantee it will be worth your time to watch him."

"I'm sure," Thomas said, shifting again. Kitty felt another urge to sneeze and in her attempts to stifle it, wound up banging against the side of the chest. Thomas immediately kicked the side of the chest, a very hard knock that raised more dust. The inside of the chest was musty, hot, and the air was getting dusty and hard to breathe. In spite of all she could do, Kitty sneezed.

"What's that?" Rachwood asked, and Thomas immediately went into a feigned sneezing fit. "Dust bothers me," Kitty heard Thomas say to Rachwood between some rather feeble sneezes.

Kitty moved to try to breathe better and hit the side of the chest again. Thomas again kicked the side, and Kitty heard Rachwood get up. "Are you all right, old man?" Rachwood asked.

"I'm having a bit of a turn," Thomas said, feigning another sneeze or two. "Captain Montfort," he called out, "I'm sorry to interrupt, but could I have a word with you."

Kitty heard Montfort curse, quite fluently, she thought, then, "I'm busy, Thomas."

Thomas moved again on the top of the chest, pretending more sneezes. "You ain't all the thing, are you? Why don't you go out for a bit of fresh air?" Rachwood asked him.

"Oh, no," Thomas said quickly, "I'm fine."

In her mind's eye, Kitty could see him. Thomas would never carry it off—prevarication just wasn't his sport. In the meantime, she was beginning to suffocate. She had visions of James finding her limp body later and weeping over it. Visions of Thomas standing dejected by her grave. She was definitely feeling the urge to sneeze again. It was too much. She knocked softly on the lid of the chest.

"What was that?" Rachwood asked, moving around.

"Just me," Thomas said. "I keep banging into this chest." There was a short pause. "Captain Montfort, I really *must* speak to you immediately."

Kitty heard Montfort stride across the floor. "Dammit, Thomas, I'm busy. This had better be urgent. That's all, Rachwood." There was a pause while Rachwood walked away, then Kitty heard Montfort speaking again. "Were you able to get Kitty out the other door and off the *Erinys?*" he asked softly.

Kitty couldn't hear Thomas's reply, but then there was an exclamation from Montfort. "Good God, man!" he yelped. "Why didn't you say so?" She heard him turn and stride across the floor away from them. "Gentlemen, there's been a slight change in plans," he said, then Kitty couldn't hear the rest. However, it was only a few moments until she heard the door open and the sound of everyone going out. She pushed on the chest, but it wouldn't give, and she felt a moment of panic. She shoved with both hands, banging against the sides and top. Then she heard Thomas. "Will you be still, Kit. For God's sake, quit that knocking around. I'll get you out just as soon as Montfort gets everyone off the boat."

True to his word, Thomas lifted the lid in just a few moments. There were candles lit in the cabin, and nothing had ever looked so good to Kitty. She stood up in the chest and breathed in deep lungfulls of air. Thomas was visibly annoyed.

"Why couldn't you stay quiet?" he demanded.

Kitty stepped out of the chest. "I'd like to see *you* stay quiet when you're hot and dusty and smothering to death," she said.

"I'd do better than you did," Thomas retorted, then, before she could reply, he took her arm. "We've got to get you back home before anyone knows you're down here. Your reputation would be entirely gone, you know, and besides, Montfort would probably strangle me if anything happened to you."

"Thomas, I want to know what's going on." Kitty tried to stand firm, but Thomas was dragging her toward the door.

"Later, Kit. For God's sake, let's just get out of here."

"Thomas, . . ."

He turned on her, furious. "I said later, Kit. We've got to go. Think what it would do to Maman if someone found you here."

"I'll tell her I was sleepwalking."

"God help me," Thomas moaned, giving her a good shove out the door. He took her hand and dragged her across the deck, then looked carefully around to see if the beach were deserted before heading across the sand.

"Thomas," Kitty said as she was dragged along behind him. "Thomas, please. I don't have on any shoes."

"My God, you walked down here *barefooted?*"

"No, I left my pattens by the dock so I wouldn't make noise walking across the deck." He was halfway up the path, pulling her along. "I could run back and get them."

"No!" The word was louder than he had intended. "I don't trust you an inch, Kitty, and you know it. You're going home and getting in your bed, and I'm going to make sure you don't move tonight. Then tomorrow I'll come back down and get your pattens. Now hurry!"

"You promised to tell me what happened." She stumbled over a stone and stopped. "Thomas, my feet hurt."

Thomas dragged her along. "I'll tell you everything later. As for your feet—you deserve anything that happens to you. Come on! With all this noise on the beach, someone is bound to come down to investigate. We'll be lucky if we can get you in the house without being found out."

From long experience, Kitty knew that Thomas in one of his stubborn moods was impossible, so she went along behind him as best as she could, complaining all the while about having to walk over stones in her bare feet. Thomas was not at all sympathetic.

To their surprise, they made it to the house without being discovered. There was a light in Papa's room and a light in the library, where they saw that Papa had dispatched a footman down to investigate. They quickly dived into the bushes and avoided him, Thomas displaying his trust of his sister by holding her down and clamping a hand over her mouth.

"That really wasn't necessary," she sputtered, when he finally decided the footman was far enough away that they could get up.

"With you, everything's necessary." Thomas got her in the back door and pushed her in front of him up the stairs. Kitty had been in her room only a moment when there was a knock at the door.

"Quick, in the bed," Thomas hissed, throwing her onto the bed and jerking up the covers. He quickly crawled behind the bed.

"Catherine, are you all right?" It was Maman.

"Fine, Maman." Kitty waited until the door opened. "What's wrong?" she managed to say, trying to pull the covers up until only her face showed.

"Nothing, I'm sure. Your father thought he heard gunshots, but I told him he was dreaming. You know how he is whenever he eats lobster patties."

"I didn't hear a thing," Kitty lied, glad that Maman couldn't see her face.

"Fine. Goodnight, dear." Maman pulled the door shut, and Thomas rolled out from behind the bed, getting up and searching for a candle. He found one and lit it. Kitty, meanwhile, had gotten out of bed.

"You might as well get yourself back in bed, because I'm going to make sure you stay right here," Thomas said.

"You don't have to do that. Just tell me what was going on, and I promise I'll stay here." She paused. "I'm too tired to move, anyway."

"So am I," Thomas said, sitting down in a chair and stretching out his legs. "I did promise, didn't I?" He looked at her and grinned. "You're absolutely dying to know, aren't you?"

Kitty grinned back at him. "You know I am, and you're enjoying this, aren't you?"

Thomas laughed, then settled back to tell her. "Kit, you wouldn't believe Montfort. This thing has been going on for weeks, and he's been right in the thick of it. He's been unbelievable."

Chapter Eighteen

Kitty punched up her pillows and leaned back. "Right in the thick of what, Thomas? The smuggling?" The word brought a bad taste to her mouth. "Are you going to be able to pay off your debts now?"

"Smuggling? Kit, will you quit riding that horse to death? Montfort has been trying to catch the smugglers, not become a smuggler himself. And guess who's been helping him?" Thomas looked at her and preened more than a little.

"He's been what?" Kitty stared at him incredulously. "I don't believe you. Not for a minute."

Thomas looked affronted. "It's true, Kit, I swear it. Montfort has an uncle who's second at the Home Office, and they were worried about this part of the country. They sent Montfort down to investigate. It seems that the locals — by that I mean Mr. Braithwaite and his cronies — had been smuggling during the war. When the peace was signed, there was no need for smuggling. So these men wanted Old Boney to come out of exile because the war was good business."

"Napoleon? What does he have to do with the smuggling?"

Thomas looked at her with a superior look. "If Napoleon was out of exile and back to fighting, the French borders would be closed to us again. There would be a huge market for smuggled goods. Just business, according to Mr. Braithwaite."

"Business? But Mr. Braithwaite isn't a smuggler."

"Oh, but yes. Looks like a cherub, doesn't he? All of which shows that you can't rely on outward appearances, as you never seem to learn."

"I never rely on outward appearances," Kitty said stiffly, her face flaming as she realized that was exactly what she had done with Montfort. "At any rate, you have to give me some credit. I did know something strange was going on."

"Yes, indeed, and you almost ruined the whole plan."

Kitty glared at him. "You could have let me in on it. I would have helped you, you know."

"Oh, yes. I can just imagine how you would have helped. Probably gone to old Braithwaite and asked him to stop immediately. As it was, we did the job." Thomas was almost crowing. "Let me tell you that Montfort was brilliant. And guess who helped him?"

"I could never guess." Thomas missed the sarcasm.

"Me." He was preening like a rooster. "We caught them red-handed, too. Turns out Braithwaite was the ringleader."

Kitty couldn't believe him. "Are you sure? Braithwaite! Not poor Barbara's father? Little, chubby Mr. Braithwaite? He seems so nice, and so concerned about Barbara."

"That little, chubby body holds a criminal mind, let me tell you. He was the brains behind all the smuggling in this area. Business, he said." Thomas snorted.

"Business? I really don't understand that. The Braithwaites seemed to have more than enough money."

"Enough to live here, probably, but he doted on that poor girl of his. Evidently he was determined to get enough money ahead to buy her a place in the *ton*. I could have told him it would never work."

"He was bound to get caught." Kitty nodded agree-

207

ment.

"Oh, no. As for the smuggling, that worked all right. What wouldn't work was buying that girl a place in London society. You know yourself that all the money in the world can't buy a place for a simpering daughter of a merchant."

"Thomas, you're being cruel," Kitty said.

"True, though, ain't it?"

Kitty looked at him for a moment, then agreed reluctantly. "Poor Barbara. I do feel for her. But, Thomas," she added, "what was all that gibberish about Napoleon?"

"That's the best part, Kit. Like I told you, Old Braithwaite and his friends wanted the war to resume because there was so much money to be made in smuggling French goods, so they had a plot going to help Napoleon get out of exile and get another army together. That's why Montfort got involved." Thomas leaned back and looked satisfied with himself. "And we scotched 'em."

Kitty sat for a moment and thought about what Thomas had said. Finally she spoke. "I feel like a complete fool, Thomas."

"Well, you acted like one for a while, but it wasn't to be helped. We knew there was no hope for it if you found out anything. Remember I did try to tell you everything was on the up and up, but you didn't believe me."

"I remember." Suddenly Kitty felt very, very tired. She leaned back against her pillows and closed her eyes. In a moment she looked at Thomas. He was yawning hugely.

"Kit, are you going to try to get out of here tonight and go snooping around again?" he asked between yawns.

She shook her head. "No, I know the story now. There's no use to investigate, is there?" She looked at Thomas who was almost asleep. "You can't manage another night in that chair, Thomas. Go on to bed, and I promise I'll stay right here."

"You promise?"

She held her fingers up in the gesture they had used in childhood. "Promise."

Thomas stood up and started for the door. "No use for you to be rambling around in the dark since everything's all done up, but I never know with you. Still, I've got to get some sleep. I don't think I've had a single good night's sleep since Montfort moved in next door." He went out, pulling her door almost shut. "Good-night, Kit, and remember you promised." With that, he shut the door and headed for his room.

Kit put on her nightrail and blew out her candle, then lay in bed thinking. She had been both right and wrong about Montfort. She had realized that her feelings for him had been changing, and that perhaps his for her had been changing as well. Surely a man didn't kiss someone the way he had kissed her if he were only trying to protect a secret. He must have some feeling for her. As far as her feelings for him . . . With a jolt, she realized that she wanted to be around him, wanted to hear him speak her name, wanted him to kiss her forever. The thought of life without him seemed unbearable.

But did he care for her in the same way? And what about Harriette? What about Richard? She dismissed the thought of Richard. She had seen tonight that she and Richard could never be suited as well as he and Marianne would be. She had known that since the moment Richard had kissed her in the garden, and she had felt nothing. She would talk with Richard tomorrow and settle that. Still, the main question was unanswered — did James care for her at all? She didn't know how to find the answer.

After much thought, accompanied by much tossing and turning, she still had no answer. It was almost daylight before she fell asleep from exhaustion.

When Kitty came downstairs, it was noon. Bidwell had spent the better part of an hour trying to repair the ravages of the night, but her eyes still looked puffy. She ate lightly and went out in search of Richard, only to discover that he was off riding. Rather than try to find him, she left word for him to come to her in the library.

It was almost midafternoon when Richard returned. He was dusty and looked almost as bad as Kitty. He came in and settled in a chair, brushing his boots. "Sorry, Kitty, but they told me you wanted to see me, and I thought it might be urgent. If it ain't, I'll go upstairs and change."

"No matter, Richard," Kitty said, drawing up a chair so she could sit and look at him while they talked. "Richard . . . ," she began.

"Don't say a thing, Kit," he interrupted. "I know what you're going to say, and I want you to know that I understand your feelings."

"You do?" Kitty was surprised. "Am I that transparent?"

"No, it's just that I realized what an oaf I was last night. I can promise you that it will never happen again. When two people make a commitment, there's no excuse for that sort of thing. It's just that . . ." He stopped and groped for words. "Dash it all, Kit, it's just that there are very few women I can talk to about putting manure on fields or dibbling in wheat." He looked at her miserably. "I know that's no excuse, and I promise I won't do it again. Once we're married, I'm sure we'll have things in common."

Kitty finally understood what he was saying. "No, Richard, you do misunderstand me. That's not what I was saying at all."

"You're not angry about me neglecting you last night?" He seemed quite bewildered.

Kitty shook her head. "No. I'm glad you did." She

reached out and took his hand. "Richard, we've known each other since leading strings and maybe that's the trouble. I think of you in the same way I think of Thomas."

He nodded. "So we'll probably rub along just fine."

"No." Kitty was having trouble keeping her temper in check. How could the man be so obtuse? "Richard, will you let me say this?"

"Certainly, Kit. I thought you were saying whatever you wanted to tell me."

She took a deep breath. "Richard, let me be blunt." She looked at him. "Richard, I love you like a brother, not the way I want to love a husband." He looked puzzled, so she continued, deciding to be perfectly plain. "Richard, I want to cry off."

He smiled broadly. "Do you mean it, Kitty?" he asked joyously, then caught himself and erased the smile. "What I mean is that, uh, I'm sorry you feel that way. It's quite a blow." His face reddened slightly at the lie, and he stumbled on. "I mean, uh, that is if you really mean to cry off, that's fine with me. I am, however, still ready to stand by our understanding."

"Don't be a goose, Richard," she said with a smile. "Anyone with half an eye can see that you're head over heels about Marianne, and that she's in love with you. You two are meant for each other, and I expect to be invited to the wedding."

"Do you think she is?" he asked. "Do you think she really cares about me?"

Kitty nodded. "Why don't you ride over to Sherbourne right now and tell her that our engagement is off? I think you may find out how much she cares."

Richard leaned over and hugged Kitty. "Kit, you're capital! No wonder Thomas is so fond of you!" With that, he stood and started to leave. "Kit, are you sure about this?"

"I'm sure," she said firmly, standing and giving him a push toward the door. "Go see Marianne."

He smiled broadly. "Kit, this is wonderful!"

His happiness was infectious. "Go on, Richard, and don't come back here until we can wish you happy."

He blew her a kiss and ran out the door.

Kitty sat wearily and leaned back in her chair, staring at the empty doorway. That was over, and now she was glad for Richard and Marianne. She and Richard would never have suited, and they had both known it. This was best for everyone; still, Kitty was surprised at the way she felt. She hadn't expected to have such an empty feeling. Without warning, she felt all alone, and for a moment had to fight off the tears that formed behind her eyes. Impatiently, she dashed them away and stood. She tried to tell herself it was all for the best, but she was unable to convince herself. In desperation, she did what she always did whenever she was upset—she went out to walk along the edge of the sea.

Richard didn't come back until very late, so Kitty didn't get to quiz him on the success of his mission. Thomas had gone to Sherbourne early, and returned early in the afternoon, but only to eat a quick meal before going off to the village to play a game of cards with some friends. As he went out the door, he casually dropped that Montfort had gone up to London to tie up some loose ends on the capture of the plotters and smugglers. Kitty managed to sound uninterested when she asked how long Montfort would be gone, and Thomas had shrugged, saying it would probably be several days, maybe even a fortnight. It was not what Kitty wanted to hear.

After a long evening spent trying to read, embroider, and various other time-killers, Kitty went to bed, still unable to sort out her feelings. She spent the next several days in a kind of limbo, not really knowing how she felt, not really wanting to analyze her feelings. Instead she tried to busy herself with reading and walking along the beach. Richard was still there, going to Sherbourne every day, so she broke the news to Papa and Maman about the understanding she and Richard had reached about their engagement. To her amazement, they seemed more relieved than anything else. Maman had sniffled about true love when Kitty told her about Richard and Marianne, but Papa had merely remarked that he knew Richard wasn't right for his Catherine all along. He and Maman got into a heated discussion on this point, so Kitty hastily grabbed her book and made her excuses.

Kit was glad she had prepared her parents because Richard made the announcement the next day that Marianne had accepted him. He was beaming with happiness, and even asked Kitty to visit Marianne, because, he said as they were eating breakfast, "Marianne is all alone over at Sherbourne now."

Kitty had raised an eyebrow. "Alone? No chaperone at all?"

"Oh, to be sure, there's an abigail with her," Richard had hastily amended. "Montfort sent for his great-aunt or some such. She's about ninety years old. All right and proper. Montfort wouldn't allow anything else."

"What happened to Miss Marlowe?" Kitty asked.

"Gone in a huff, the day after she and Montfort had some sort of disagreement. I thought I told you."

"No, Richard, you didn't." Kitty thought a moment, and then decided that a direct question was the best route with Richard. "Richard, what about the engagement between Harriette and Montfort? Is that off?"

Richard speared a currant cake and spread it with butter. "Never was on, as far as I can tell. From what

Marianne's let drop, I think that was all in Harriette's head."

"But Harriette told me the announcement was all ready. She was posting it to her father."

Richard spread jam on the other half of the currant cake. "Maybe she was, but I don't think Montfort knew anything about it. I think Harriette planned to force his hand by having everything ready. She didn't think he would disgrace the family or some such if she forced it. She should have known that nobody forces a chap like Montfort to do anything he don't want to do." Richard ate the cake in two big bites. "And Montfort didn't want to marry that chit, that's for sure."

"Are you sure?" Kitty held her breath.

Richard looked at her, startled. "Of course I'm sure. After all, Marianne told me so. Told me that Montfort would probably never get married."

"Never? Why?" Kitty felt faint.

"I don't know. Married to the army or the Home Office or some such muck. That's what he told Harriette, at any rate." Richard started to take another currant cake, then settled for eggs and a muffin.

"I'm going home today, Kit," he said between bites. "Got to get all this wedding business straightened out, you know. Need to tell my father all about the change in fiancées. I thought it would be best to tell him rather than try to write. I never was much of a hand with a letter, and I was afraid he'd be all confused by all the goings-on here." He pushed his plate away and concentrated on his tea. "One thing, though, Kit. Would you keep Marianne company while I'm gone? I know she'd love to have another woman to talk to. That old harridan Montfort sent down to stay with her is deaf as a post, so she don't signify. Anyway, you ought to enjoy going over there—women like to talk weddings and so on, don't they?"

"It's my favorite thing," Kitty said with sarcasm, but it was completely wasted on Richard.

"Capital! I knew you'd do it, Kit," he said, finishing his tea. "I'm going to run over there before I leave and tell Marianne. Perhaps you could go over this afternoon. I don't want her to get lonesome."

"That would never do."

Richard nodded agreement and gave her a sisterly kiss on the cheek before he left. "You're really capital, Kit, or have I told you that before?" With that, he was out the door.

Kit sat and absently stirred her chocolate. Thomas came in while she sat here. He was yawning hugely. "Late evening with the card players, Thomas?" she couldn't resist asking maliciously.

"What's the matter, Kit? Moping over losing Richard to Marianne, eh?" He took a seat as Kitty glared at him. "Story of your life, Kit. First you lose old Albert or Alfred or whatever to Harriette, and now you lose a prime 'un like Richard to Marianne." He gave her a wicked grin. "Don't look as if we're ever going to get you married off."

Kitty gritted her teeth. "I've decided to be an old maid. I plan to be into caps within the year. Just as soon as I can get some made." She slammed down her spoon and threw her serviette over Thomas's head.

He laughed, removing the napkin. "Do you know what you need, Kit?"

"No, but I'm sure you're going to tell me."

"Quite right. You need a trip to London. Just the ticket for getting a girl out of the mopes."

"Balderdash."

"Say whatever you want to, but I think it would do you a world of good. I'm going up first of the week and you can go with me."

"And no doubt put up with some opera dancer of your

acquaintance? That *would* do me a world of good."

Thomas shook his head and looked offended. "Lord, Kit, give me some credit. I was going to stay at Aunt Het's, and I'm sure she'd be glad to have you there too."

"I don't know." Kit sat and thought about it. It did sound better than rusticating in the country talking to Marianne about weddings, dibbling wheat, and manuring fields.

"I'll even take you around town," Thomas offered as Kit gave him an astonished look. "Well," he said sheepishly as he saw her expression. "You ain't half bad looking, you know. I don't mind being seen with you."

"For that, I thank you, Thomas. I don't know any girl who has a better brother." He caught her sarcasm and had the grace to blush.

"Come on, Kit, I'm trying to be nice. It ain't exactly something I'm very good at."

"Obviously." She thought for a moment. "Why are you going up to London?"

Thomas waved his fork at her. "Montfort's going to be up there for a while and wanted me to come up and meet some people. Don't say anything to Maman and Papa, because I want to surprise them, but I think I may get a position at the Home Office out of this thing."

"You? At the Home Office?" Kitty choked on the words.

Thomas looked pained. "And what's wrong with that? Montfort seems to think I'd do a fine job. Told me so."

"Montfort." She looked at him. "No doubt you'll be with Montfort the whole time we're in London."

"So you are going." He looked at her with satisfaction. "I knew you would when I mentioned that. Well, I know how you feel about Montfort, and you'll never have a better chance of having him around."

Kitty stared at him. "And what do you mean by that?"

"Come on, Kit. I've seen how the wind blows there.

What I'm doing is giving you a chance to do something about it. Matchmaker that I am, I thought I'd get you in London and Montfort in London, then see what happened."

"You did such a wonderful job with Richard and me."

Thomas laughed. "At any rate, if I hadn't invited Richard here, he would never have met Marianne. You have to admit that."

"Matchmaking by default," Kitty said, joining in his laughter.

"I was leaving for London day after tomorrow. Can you be ready by then? I can write Aunt Het and post it today so she'll be expecting both of us." He gave her his engaging smile that never affected her. This time, though, she saw why other women were so gullible when Thomas smiled.

"All right, Thomas. But *no* matchmaking." She got up and headed for the door. "I'm going to London only to spend a few days shopping."

Thomas watched her go out, a smile on his face. "In a pig's eye," he said.

Chapter Nineteen

Aunt Het welcomed them effusively when they arrived. Maman had decided to come to London with them since Kitty had told her she was going to do some shopping. Thomas was not overly pleased to have Maman along, but once her mind was made up, there was no stopping her.

Thomas deposited the two of them with Aunt Het and all their luggage, then made a hasty retreat. "Need to check in on some urgent business," he yelled over his shoulder as he leaped over the portmanteaux and hurried out the door.

"A likely story," Kitty muttered after him, then was smothered again in Aunt Het's embrace as her aunt spent several minutes telling her how outmoded her clothes were, and congratulating Maman on finally getting Kitty to London to be outfitted in the latest. For the first time, Kitty was overjoyed when Bidwell arrived in the second carriage and whisked her off upstairs to rest.

The next few days were a whirlwind of shopping and sending out and receiving cards. Aunt Het and Maman seemed to have put their heads together to fill up every second of Kitty's days. From hints Aunt Het dropped, Kit thought they had also plotted to introduce her to every eligible bachelor in London.

There was, unfortunately, only one bachelor she wished to see, and he had been elusive. Not one glimpse had she had of Montfort, and Thomas was a singularly silent conspirator. Montfort had set up an interview at the Home Office for Thomas on Thursday afternoon, and the poor boy spent the entire week in a state of nervous agitation. Kit tried to cheer him up, but there was nothing for it. In desperation, on Tuesday, she even suggested he go out with one of his previous *amours*. Thomas merely glared at her. "A man in government can't afford a hint of scandal," he said loftily.

Kit wasn't successful in hiding her giggles, and Thomas was quite put out. "Dash it all, Kit. Don't you know how much rests on this interview? Montfort seems to think it will go well, but you know me — if it can be bungled, I'll do it." He sat down dejectedly on the sofa.

"Thomas, don't be silly. You'll be perfectly splendid." She looked down at him. "As long, of course, as you don't wear that horrid pea-green waistcoat."

Thomas looked down at his maligned garment. "True. It looks as if I'm going to lose that wager to Richard. Never thought I'd see the day I'd lose my touch with waistcoats. I can't even do that right any more." He looked in positive despair. "I could have carried this off last season."

Kit sat beside him. "Don't be an idiot, Thomas. No one could carry off a waistcoat that looks like pond scum." She hesitated a moment. "I know you've seen Ja . . . Captain Montfort. Um, what is he doing?"

"Well, he ain't squiring Harriette Marlowe around, that's for sure." Thomas looked at her. "You're dead serious about him, aren't you, Kit?" he asked. "I thought so, but I wasn't really sure."

Kitty avoided looking at him. "I don't know how he feels."

"But you are serious about him?"

Kitty hesitated and her face flamed red. It was impossible to utter her feelings.

"I see," Thomas said thoughtfully. Then he put his hand on hers. "We're a pair, ain't we, Kit? Me in a tizzy about a position with the Home Office, and you in a dither about Montfort."

Kitty sighed. "There's hardly anything I can do, Thomas. I can't very well go chasing out in the streets looking for him. For you it's different, though. If you really want that government position, you should go after it. Why don't you practice with me?"

He looked at her strangely, then laughed. "Always right to the point, Kit. All right, that's a good idea. I'll write out the questions I think will be asked, and then we'll practice." He rose and went to the desk, whistling, then left with quill and paper in hand. Kitty leaned back on the sofa, relieved. If things weren't any better for her, at least Thomas was in a better humor.

And practice they did. Every second that Kitty wasn't out shopping, she was with Thomas asking him questions over and over, even adding some of her own. Finally, by Wednesday night, he thought he had his answers well down.

His appointment was for two on Thursday, and Kitty was on tenterhooks until he came home. "Well?" she asked breathlessly as he came through the door. He looked at her closely. To Kitty it seemed he had aged five years since he had left at noon. He seemed older, more settled. "I don't know. I think I answered everything satisfactorily, and, of course, Montfort had put in a good word for me. I just have to wait and see."

Kitty grimaced. "In the meantime, we have to get ready for that squeeze at the Alfords."

"Oh, Lord, Kit. I had completely forgotten it. Do you think I could come down with a convenient ailment?"

"You might get by, but don't try a headache. I was going to use that one."

He looked at her and grinned. "I certainly will use it.

By the way, Montfort's going to be at the Alfords. Said he was going in late."

"Then perhaps I should leave early," Kitty said. "If he can't come see me, I certainly don't intend to throw myself at him."

Thomas grinned wickedly at her. "As you told me, if you want something, you have to go after it. And, since Richard has broadcast far and wide that you proposed to him, I'm sure Montfort wouldn't take it amiss . . ."

"Richard what! He wouldn't. I did no such thing!"

Thomas laughed uproariously, looking and acting like his usual self. "Got you, didn't I, Kit?" He stopped laughing and looked at her. "I am serious, though, about you letting Montfort know that you might be, ah, interested. Nothing pushy like Harriette, but you could let him know."

Kitty blushed as she recalled Montfort's kisses. "I believe he already knows."

Thomas looked at her, then took her hand. "Get ready to go to the Alfords, and I'll go plead my headache. We'll talk about this later."

Maman and Aunt Het made sure that Thomas had a tray sent up to his room and left instructions for him to get a good night's rest. The three ladies went on to the Alfords' squeeze, which Kitty found to be a dead bore. There were people she had met in her previous season, people she hadn't met, and people she never wished to meet again. She did see Harriette Marlowe there, fanning herself and making coquette's eyes at an older man in uniform. Kitty walked by Harriette, who made a point of turning away and giving her the cut direct. Kitty chuckled audibly.

Maman came up to Kitty through the press of people. "This heat has given me the headache, Kitty," she said, and truly she was looking pale. "I had hoped to stay and let you meet some of your acquaintances, but I must go.

You may stay with Het if you wish."

Kitty shook her head. "No, I'd rather leave." Much relieved, she went over and left word for their carriage to be brought around.

In the carriage, Aunt Het was much agog over news of Harriette Marlowe. "I heard she had Sobey's boy on the hook, but he got away. Now she's dangling after some Russian officer. Her father's fit to be tied." Aunt Het was obviously quite satisfied with the news.

Once home, Maman and Aunt Het inquired about Thomas and were told that he was resting, so they went up to their chambers. Kit wasn't really that sleepy, so she threw her shawl down and wandered into Aunt Het's library, a large room that was used more for card playing than for reading. She was browsing among the little-used books when she heard the knocker. In just a moment, the butler came to the door to ask if she would receive a visitor. She nodded yes and, to her surprise, Montfort came through the door.

"Catherine," he said, and the name sounded like wind in the leaves.

"Captain Montfort." She sounded stiff even to her ears.

He walked across the floor to her. "How have you been?" He was as formal as she. "I stopped by to leave word with Thomas that he has been accepted for the position with the Home Office."

Kitty broke into a smile. "That's wonderful. And thank you for your help."

"I did very little. Thomas is a remarkable young man."

"Perhaps I know him too well," Kitty said dryly.

"Most sisters do," he answered, then they stood awkwardly, not saying anything.

The words she had used to help Thomas came back to Kitty—"If you want something, you have to go after it."

The trouble was, she didn't know how to start. She looked at Montfort as the silence lengthened.

"I'd hoped to see you in London. Thomas told me you were here," he said.

Kitty looked into his eyes. They were dark, the candle picking up the golden glints in them. "I had hoped to see you as well," she said, taking a deep breath. In for a penny, in for a pound, she thought to herself. "I wanted to apologize to you. I was entirely wrong about you, and I'm sorry. I should have known better."

"You certainly should have," he said promptly, then laughed at her expression. "I don't think you were entirely wrong, though."

"I thought you were a rogue and a scoundrel," Kitty said, looking at him and not being able to catch her breath.

"Maybe I am," he said, coming closer to her and touching her face with his fingertips. "Would it make a difference?" Before she could answer, he was kissing her, kissing her in the way she had dreamed of, his kisses making her feel giddy and weak. "Catherine," he said again, as his lips moved down her throat.

She stepped back, trying to control her emotions. He moved back as well. "I'm sorry," he said. "I didn't mean to do that."

Kitty licked her bruised lips. You have to go after what you want, she had said to Thomas. "Do you care about me, James?" she asked.

A soft smile touched his face. "Do you need to ask me that, Catherine? The answer should be obvious."

"I want to hear it. Do you care at all for me?"

"Yes, I care very much."

Kitty closed her eyes and took a deep breath. "James, I don't know how we would do together, but perhaps . . ." She started all over again. "James, I know we don't seem very similar, but there are times when two people . . ."

She stopped again.

"Good heavens," Montfort said, coming close to her again. "Is this a proposal, my dear Miss Walsingham? Are you on the verge of offering for me?"

Kitty looked into his eyes. "Yes," she said. "Will you marry me, James?"

He laughed aloud and took her into his arms. "Yes, yes, a thousand times yes. I've wanted to ask you the same question a dozen times, but wondered if the time would ever be right. I should have known you'd get straight to the point."

"Yes, you will?" Kitty couldn't believe her ears.

He kissed her lightly. "Yes, my poppet. And no, we probably won't rub along together at times, but I guarantee life with you will never be dull."

There was a muffled chuckle from the depths of the sofa, and Kitty and James sprang apart. Thomas sat up and peered over the back of the sofa. "You've been there all along," Kitty cried. "That wasn't being much of a gentleman, Thomas!"

"Lord, Kit, you know I ain't ever been much of a gentleman." He stood up and laughed. "Looks as if we both got what we came to London for—I got a position at the Home Office and you got Montfort." He paused before he went out the door. "I'd say I got the better bargain."

Montfort looked at Thomas and chuckled as he left, then turned back to Kitty and took her into his arms again. His eyes were almost golden with love.

"Did you come to London for me? Really?" he asked.

"I certainly did," Kitty said, "and don't you believe Thomas for a minute. I think you got the better bargain."

"I know I did, my sweet," he said, kissing her lightly. "And I intend to keep it forever."

"I intend to make sure you do," Kitty said with a smile as she reached up and pulled his dark head down to hers.